Karen gasped in horror as she saw her son crumple to the ground. Instantly, she flew at the motorcycle driver, like a lioness protecting her cubs. These barbarians were not going to make her cower in fear, she thought. She had no idea that this one act of defiance would start a war . . . a war that could threaten the lives of the very loved ones she was so anxious to protect.

Series Story Editor **Mary Ann Cooper** is America's foremost soap opera expert. She writes the nationally syndicated column *Speaking of Soaps*, is a major contributor to leading soap opera magazines, and has appeared as a guest on numerous radio and television talk shows.

Scott Cunningham, author of *Misguided Hearts*, is an experienced screen writer who currently resides in California.

Dear Friend,

We all gain a certain sense of security from places we find most familiar. The women of Knots Landing felt that their private beach party would be the perfect diversion on a sultry summer day. The screech and roar of motor-cycles shattered the calm of the afternoon and shook the peaceful community to its very roots. No one in Knots Landing would feel quite so safe again—not as long as brazen hoodlums roamed their streets to harass and intimidate all who would oppose them.

Still, Sid Fairgate was never one to back down. In Book 4 of the *Soaps & Serials* Knots Landing book series, the Fairgates face unknown dangers as they stand up for what they believe in—a safer world.

For Soaps & Serials Books,

Mary Ann Cooper

Mary Ann Cooper

P.S. If you missed *Soaps & Serials's* earlier novelizations of KNOTS LANDING and can't find them in your local book source, please see the order form inserted in the back of this book.

KNOTS LANDING™

4

Misguided Hearts

From the television series created by David Jacobs

PIONEER COMMUNICATIONS NETWORK, INC.

Misguided Hearts

From the television series KNOTS LANDING™
created by David Jacobs. This book is based on
scripts written by Robert Gilmer and Clyde Ware.

KNOTS LANDING™ paperback novels are
published and distributed by Pioneer
Communications Network, Inc.

SOAPS & SERIALS™ is a trademark of Pioneer
Communications Network, Inc.

ISBN: 0-916217-64-7

Printed in the United States of America

10 9 8 7 6 5 4 3 2 1

Misguided Hearts

Chapter One

Small Surprise

Karen Fairgate sat poised on the cold chair in the doctor's waiting room, legs crossed, hands perched on her lap. She examined the badly painted seascape that hung over the vinyl couch opposite her.

How could I have gotten myself into this mess? She frowned. Did I forget something? Is this an act of God? How could this be happening to me, at *my age*?

A blonde, fleshy pregnant woman, whose belly pushed against her pink maternity blouse, fanned herself with an issue of Family Circle while shifting from side to side on the couch.

"Hot today," she said with a pleasant smile.

"Yes," Karen agreed, then turned away.

"It's always hot when you're pregnant," observed the woman.

A nurse's head appeared from behind a sliding pane of glass which separated the office from the waiting room. "Mrs. Klinger, Dr. Bender will see

7

you now. Will you come this way, please?''

''It's about time,'' the pregnant woman groaned. She leaned forward, legs widely splayed, planted her feet on the floor, then, leading with her stomach, rose from the chair and shuffled through the door past a tight-skirted nurse.

When she was alone in the waiting room Karen sighed. This is all so ridiculous, she thought. What am *I* doing here? I must have been mistaken.

The front door to the offices of Dr. Louise Bender, OB/GYN, opened, momentarily shooting a slice of brilliant California sunshine into the room. A slim woman walked in, stopped in the doorway, then stepped forward.

''Karen! Hi, neighbor!'' a familiar voice said.

''Hello, Ginger.''

Ginger Ward, young, attractive, and wide-eyed, pecked Karen's cheek as she sat beside her. ''I'm surprised to see you here,'' she said. ''What's up? You and Sid planning something that you haven't told me about?''

''No,'' Karen answered quietly. ''Just a checkup. How about you?''

Ginger paused, pursed her lips, then shrugged. ''Same here.''

Karen snapped her fingers, half-smiling. ''I thought I might be the first one in the circle to hear the good news.''

Ginger shook her head, sending her brown hair flying. ''No. There's nothing to hear—darn it!''

Karen straightened in her chair. ''I'm sorry to hear that, Ginger. Are you and Kenny trying?''

She looked at Karen frankly. "We are and we aren't. It's hard to explain."

"Oh, come on, Ginger," Karen said. "You're either trying to have a baby or you're not. Which is it?"

"I guess you could say that we are trying, frequently. That is, *I'm* trying."

"You are?"

"That's right. But Kenny doesn't know about it." Ginger held Karen's gaze.

"You mean you—"

Ginger nodded. "He hasn't found out yet." She exhaled loudly and slumped back into her chair.

"Does Kenny want children?" Karen asked.

Ginger narrowed her eyes. "I don't know. He keeps saying he's not ready. He's *never* ready, and I'm tired of waiting for him."

"I can't blame you, if you want a baby," Karen said.

"I do."

"So you . . . took steps?"

She nodded.

"But no luck so far?"

Ginger shook her head. "No. Dr. Bender says it's too soon to assume that there's anything wrong with Kenny or me. We've just had bad luck. I guess we'll have to keep trying."

Karen touched Ginger's arm. "Hey, at least it's fun trying."

Ginger grinned.

The nurse appeared again. "Mrs. Fairgate?"

Karen stood, steeling herself for the news. "Wish me luck," she said, then bit off the words.

Ginger's eyebrows lifted. "What are you

talking about? I thought you were here for a checkup. Karen, something's not wrong with you, is it? You would have told me, right?'' She gripped Karen's arm.

''I'm fine, really,'' Karen assured her.

''Mrs. Fairgate?'' the nurse repeated.

''See you later, Ginger,'' Karen said. She slid out from the woman's grip and turned toward the nurse. Following her through the door and into Dr. Bender's office, Karen prepared herself. Please, she prayed to anyone who would hear— please let me have been mistaken.

''Hello, Mrs. Fairgate,'' Dr. Bender rose from her chair. The doctor was young, somewhat stocky, and appealingly open.

''Hello, Dr. Bender,'' Karen's voice was low as she walked into the panelled office.

''Please, sit down.''

''Thank you.''

''Your husband's not here?'' she said, glancing around.

Karen smiled nervously. ''He's at work. Dr. Bender, could you please just tell me the results?'' she asked anxiously.

''Of course,'' Dr. Bender shuffled through Karen's files. ''Lab work. Ah, here it is.'' She studied the paper for a moment, then glanced up at Karen. ''Mrs. Fairgate, you're going to be a mother.''

Oh no, Karen thought. Her throat tightened and she gripped the chair's arms, her fingers stiff. ''Are you saying . . .''

''You're pregnant, Mrs. Fairgate. You're going to have a baby.'' Dr. Bender's expression was neutral.

Karen trembled as her nostrils flared from the tension. Don't think about it, don't think about it, she told herself. Relax.

Dr. Bender touched Karen's shoulder. Karen's body jerked at the contact.

"Mrs. Fairgate, I've seen women faint, scream, burst into tears or sit quietly smiling after I've told them the news, but you seem almost dazed. Are you okay?"

Karen looked up at the doctor, her cheeks tingling with red. "I'm sorry, Dr. Bender. This is such a shock."

"I take it you weren't planning this pregnancy."

"You take it right." She shook her head. "I was so sure I was wrong."

"Then it's a good thing you came in to take the test," Dr. Bender said. "Take some time to absorb this news, and remember that you can contact me with any questions you might have."

Karen looked up mutely at the doctor.

The doctor leaned forward in her chair. "Take some time," she repeated, her voice compassionate. "Meanwhile, we'll start you on prenatal care."

"Whatever you say," Karen replied in a toneless voice. She stared at the wall. How could it be? *How could it be?*

"Mrs. Fairgate?" the doctor questioned.

Karen roused herself. "I'm sorry—I'm being foolish. I'm in shock." Her smile was faint. "Thanks, Dr. Bender. I'll call to make an appointment."

"Fine. And call me if you need any information."

Karen's eyes were moist as she turned from the doctor and walked into the waiting room. A quick glance told her that Ginger wasn't in sight. Grateful that she didn't have to face her friend, Karen slipped out of the office in a near-trance.

Outside, the lustrous California sunshine didn't lighten her mood as she mechanically walked to her station wagon, got in and turned the ignition. Her hands worked automatically as she backed out of the parking space and pulled onto the tree-lined street.

Karen opened the window, then leaned her head slightly toward the rush of cool air that billowed in through the opening. It isn't true, she told herself without conviction. I can't be pregnant. The lab must have made a mistake. Is it possible that now, in my thirty-seventh year, I'll bear a fourth child?

Karen shook her head. What would Sid say, and the kids? Her husband would probably welcome it, love the idea, but the kids . . . Diana, Eric and Michael were something else altogether.

The thought of her family began to melt her stony mood. The initial shock thinned out like fog in morning sun. A feeling of warmth and new possibilities engulfed her. Karen tingled as she drove.

I'm going to have a baby. Karen smiled as she thought it. In seven or eight months there'll be a new Fairgate in the house, bawling his head off all night, demanding more attention than anyone else, disrupting and changing our lives forever, like any child.

I'm going to have a baby. Karen dared to

believe the words. Her mind flashed back to earlier pregnancies, to the joys and pains of birthing and raising three children.

Karen stopped at a red light beside a flower stand. She glanced at the car next to her. A young woman sat behind the wheel, pulling her hair back with one hand while talking to the young child on the seat beside her. In the back a baby sat strapped inside a child seat.

Two children—at *her* age, Karen marveled. She couldn't be more than eighteen. I can't imagine having that much responsibility so young.

The light changed. As she drove Karen watched the people around her—there seemed to be a plethora of mothers and mothers-to-be in Knots Landing that morning. A pregnant woman walked into a baby furnishings store; another quickly pushed a stroller across a busy street, while a third helped her one-year old move along on his toddling feet.

Babies everywhere, Karen thought, and then looked down at her flat stomach. Could it be true? Could she be pregnant?

A sharp honk from behind her induced Karen to speed up slightly. She had dropped to below fifteen miles per hour. A willowy girl on a bicycle with a baby in the basket over the front wheel sailed past her car. A *young* woman, Karen noticed ruefully.

They were young, all of them. Every mother she'd seen. Young women were supposed to have babies. It was natural. The older a woman is, she remembered Dr. Bender telling her once, the more risks she takes with childbirth.

She thought of her husband again. Karen

envisioned herself telling him the news by walking into the bedroom and casually saying, "Sid, what are you doing for the next eighteen years?"

Would he want another child? Karen's mind flooded with questions and doubts. What would Sid really say? What would her children think? And what did *she* think? How did *she* feel?

Karen flipped on the radio. Mellow music drifted from the speakers, but Karen couldn't drown her questions in the music. One question in particular wouldn't die: what would Sid think if she told him she didn't want another baby? What would he say to an abortion?

Five motorcycles wound along the ocean-front road, their huge engines screaming as they passed miles of rugged coastline. Firmly astride the largest machine, a big long-haired, gray-bearded biker glanced at his buddy. "Hey, Music!" he yelled over the engines' noise.

Music, clean-shaven, ruggedly handsome, with three-inch-long brown hair, smiled at his friend. "What, Alien?" he shouted back.

"Let's pull over." He gestured to the side of the road.

Music nodded and signaled the riders behind him. The two lead bikes slowly reduced their speed as they veered to the right and rolled onto the gravel shoulder. Alien squeezed his brakes and spun a 360-degree circle on the dirt.

"You're still crazy, Alien," Music laughed.

The other three bikers pulled up behind them.

"Hey Music, why're we stoppin'?" a rail-thin, sandy-blond man asked.

"Cause we are, Ross."

"All right, all right." Ross lit a cigarette and wandered off the road.

A strangely attractive woman, her hair dyed a little too black, climbed off a motorcycle, pushing up provocatively against the leather-clad back of its driver. She walked up to Music. "Got any beer?" she asked, flapping her eyelashes.

"Yeah." Music grabbed one from the pack on his bike and threw it to her. "Catch!" he said, laughing.

Mary grabbed it, grinned, and walked off.

"Hey man, when're we gettin' to Laguna?" Alien brushed off his hands as he sat on his bike.

"I don't know. Soon, I guess. The rest of them are already there, but I'm in no big hurry." He pulled a pack of cigarettes from his leather jacket, stuck one between his lips, and struck a light. He sucked in deeply. "Hey, look at that!" Music pointed.

Through the intermittent trees and brush alongside the road they saw Alison, their other female companion, walk up to where Ross was quietly sitting under a tree. He threw his cigarette down, grabbed her and pulled her to the ground.

Music snorted. "I had a feeling about those two."

"Alison and Ross?" Alien asked. "I can't see it."

Music sat perched on his bike as Alien broke out more of the nearly-cold beers. He threw one to Music who caught it and, in one clean motion, opened the can. Suds spurted out, splashing Music's face and leather jacket.

"First bath you've had in weeks, dude," Alien laughed. "No wonder Alison hooked up with Ross."

"Cut the crap, Alien." Music wasn't smiling. "Hey, I can get any woman I want. I got the style and the looks."

Alien guffawed.

"Shut up," Music snapped.

"Sure. Go ahead. The next foxy chick you see, grab her."

Music shook his head. "Man, I'm tired of all this road work. I wanna have some fun, man! This is too damn boring." He glanced at Alien, who now also sat on his bike. "What's the next town we hit?"

He mused, scratching his beard. "Knots Landing, I think. Why?"

"No reason," Music replied. "Just thought we could stir up some trouble there. Might break up the monotony."

"Sure," Alien said. "Why not?" He wandered off into the brush.

"Music!" a feminine voice called.

He turned and looked. He was alone. Ross, Allison, Alien and the other bikers were nowhere in sight. It must be Mary.

"I'm right here!" she said unseen.

"Damn it, Mary, quit playing games." He took a drag off his cigarette. What the hell did she want?

"Come here."

He followed the voice past a tree. Beyond it he found Mary stretched out on the dried leaves beneath a massive oak. Her tee-shirt clung to her from the heat. Mary's hand moved languidly in a

16

line from her chin down to the waist-band of her jeans.

"I heard you say something about stirring up some trouble." Her voice was husky. "How about stirring some up with me?"

"It's been a long time, Mary," Music said.

"I know," she sighed. "We just didn't get along. But I need a man *now*, Music . . . I need a man—but you'll do until one comes along."

Music stuck his hands on his hips as he approached the woman. "Mary, you never change, do you?" He knelt. Music's hands thrust out and locked around the woman's wrists. "You're some fox, you know that?"

Mary struggled to break free. "Let me go, Music! You know I'm just kidding. Come on, man!"

Music let her fall onto the leaves and sauntered off.

"You've got a serious attitude problem, Music!" Mary yelled.

He laughed and walked back to his bike, puffing on the smoke, then threw it down and ground the butt beneath his boot. Attitude problem? Hell no, Music thought. He's got the best attitude he can have. What Music wants, Music gets.

The biker smiled as he remembered past conquests. Loving a woman was almost better than riding his hog.

"Come back, Music!" Mary said. "You know I wasn't *really* kidding! Come on, we'll have some fun. Music!"

He shrugged and pulled off his leather jacket, threw it onto his motorcycle, and went back to the bushes where he'd left Mary.

She was gone.

"Mary?"

Suddenly she was on top of him, all legs and arms and scratching nails. The fox climbed the tree, Music thought as he bent and flipped her off his back. Mary laughed as she sprang to her feet before him.

"Ready for another round?"

"Damn it, Mary. Sometimes I think you forget you're a woman."

Mary arched her back. "As long as you never forget, Music." She turned and walked away.

He looked at his bike, then went to it and stroked its gas tank. It was the only "she" he'd ever trusted.

Chapter Two
Land of the Free

The Pacific Ocean lapped at the edge of Knots Landing beach, its perfectly rounded waves glistening in the hot afternoon sun. The scent of coconut oil mixed with the aroma of roasting hotdogs and the salty odor of the sea.

Karen Fairgate stretched out in her beach chair far up on the sand and adjusted the left shoulder strap of her one piece bathing suit. The warm sun and the swellings of the sea were soothing, almost hypnotic. She stretched again and sat up.

Her daughter Diana had joined a collection of eight teenagers at a net stretched across the beach for an impromptu volleyball game. As Karen watched, Diana sprang up beside the net and slam-dunked the ball on the opposite side.

"Great shot!" Karen yelled, clapping delightedly. Her daughter was oblivious to Karen's praise.

"What?" Val Ewing lifted her eyes from the cold soda in her hands.

19

"Nothing," Karen said. "Diana just made a good shot in the volleyball game."

"Oh." Val gazed at the water where Laura Avery and Ginger Ward were teaching Laura's seven-year-old son Jason to swim. They splashed in knee-deep surges of water.

"Doesn't it look good out there? So cool and refreshing?" Karen savored the sight.

Val shrugged. "I guess."

"Wouldn't you like to find out?"

"Maybe someday . . ." she hesitated.

"How can you come out to the beach and not swim?" Karen prodded "It's not normal."

"I'm not ready to learn how yet, I guess." Val took a swallow from the gleaming aluminum can.

A Frisbee sailed perilously close over their heads.

"You gotta move faster," Eric Fairgate shouted, as his younger brother stumbled after the wayward Frisbee.

"You threw it too high!" Michael complained, rolling on the sand in youthful exuberance.

"Eric! Michael!" Karen yelled. "Don't throw that thing over here! You nearly hit us!"

Michael, disc in hand, turned to face his mother. "He threw it too hard, Mom!"

"He just can't catch," his sibling accused, moving toward him.

"I don't care how hard you throw it or how lousy a catch you are," Karen scolded. "Just don't do it in this direction."

"Okay," Michael grumbled. "But it's not my fault."

Eric ran full tilt toward his younger brother.

Michael stared at him momentarily, then realizing the boy wasn't going to stop, ran to his mother.

Eric easily grabbed the Frisbee from his brother's hand, jogged twenty yards past him, then spun and shot the disc hard and high toward his twelve-year-old brother.

"Mom!" the boy cried.

Karen turned toward her son's call automatically, but her eyes quickly left the typical scene of sibling rivalry. Diana, bouncing through the course of two volleyball games, had nearly bounced out of her bikini top. The tiny strap stretched low across Diana's upper left arm. One more slam-dunk and Karen's sixteen-year-old daughter would be on public display.

"Mom!" Michael cried again.

"Eric, cut it out!" she yelled, not turning her eyes from Diana. As she held her breath the ball flew across the court toward her daughter. She was being set up for a shot.

Karen watched tensely as Diana, in continuous motion, slammed the ball over the net and yanked up the top of her bathing suit.

Karen smiled and exhaled, then turned. Eric and Michael were running peacefully now along the shallows, their ankles cutting exaggerated swathes through the water.

"Karen, are you feeling okay?" Valene asked, "You've been acting kinda peculiar all afternoon."

Karen smiled and turned to Val. "I'm fine, really."

"Come on." Val was not convinced. "I know when things aren't right. You can't fool me."

"No, honestly, Val. There's nothing to talk about."

Valene finished her soda. "Ginger said something about running into you at Dr. Bender's today," she said with concern.

"So?" Karen replied, shooting a look at her. "Just a routine checkup. You see her too," she pointed out.

"*Everyone* sees Dr. Bender." Val fixed her eyes on Karen's face and frowned. "That's not what I'm talking about, and you know it."

"What do you mean, Val?" Karen asked.

Val paused. "Never mind. Sorry I brought it up. I was just worried."

"Nothing to be worried about," Karen touched Val's shoulder. She stood and stared at the waves, then suddenly turned back to Val with a grin. "That does it."

"That does *what*?"

"D-Day!"

"What are you talking about?" Val asked, running her fingers through the baking sand beside her. "D for what?"

"Dunk!" Karen grabbed Val's arms. "Time to get that bathing suit of yours broken in!" She tried to pull Val from the beach chair.

"On your feet!"

"Oh, no!" Val cried. "I can't. I mean . . ." She held onto the chair's arms, jokingly fighting off Karen's hands.

"Come on! You said you wanted to learn how to swim. You told me that yourself. So what's the problem?"

"I want to learn how to swim—yes, but in a pool, not the Pacific Ocean!"

Karen dragged Val to her feet and then half-pulled her down toward the surf. Ginger and Laura turned to watch as Val's toes hit the surf.

"You've been living in Knots Landing for months now, Val Ewing," Karen said, "and salt water hasn't even touched your knees. It's ridiculous, and I'm not going to stand for it!" Karen escorted Val further into the water, one hand on her waist, the other holding her wrist.

"It's so cold!" Val screeched, her face alive with fear and excitement.

"Look at that! Jason's really picking it up."

The young boy paddled doggy-style, bright-eyed but barely keeping his sputtering mouth above water. He was obviously enjoying himself immensely as he swam around Ginger's and Laura's legs.

"Oh, all right," Val said. "If you're going to make such a big deal about it, go right ahead."

"You're a natural born swimmer, Val, if I've ever seen one," Laura called, as she splashed toward Karen and Val, with Ginger and a half-submerged Jason in tow.

"Don't make me nervous," Val watched as a wave approached her. As it broke ten feet from her, spray whipped around and over the women.

"Those waves are awful big." Val shuddered.

"Whatever you do," Karen instructed, holding Val's hand in the surf as the water churned around their ankles and rolled back in preparation for another wave, "don't turn your back on the ocean. You never know when a big one'll creep up on you. If you're facing the water you can see the waves coming. Then you have time to decide whether to jump or dive into them.''

"Dive? *Into* waves?" Val's face grew pale. Her eyes narrowed, and she tried to shrug out of Karen's grip. "I—I think I need another soda," she said.

"Come on," Ginger urged her. "We haven't even started."

"I think I'm finished." Val shook off Karen's hand and turned to start back for the beach.

A wall of irridescent water four feet high thundered down onto the beach. The force of the waves pushed the other women around, and Jason's head went under momentarily, but Val fell. She tumbled into the foaming water, arms and hair adrift.

"Val!" Karen screamed as she flapped toward her.

The wave expended itself on the sand and withdrew rapidly. Val sat up, coughing and rubbing her eyes.

"Are you all right?" Karen asked as the three women huddled around Val.

She opened her eyes and looked up at them, coughed, then put out a hand for help. Once on her feet Val Ewing sniffled and held Karen's arm for support.

"I must have swallowed half the Pacific," she moaned

"Val, I'm sorry I forced you into this," Karen said, her face grave.

Val laughed. "Heck, Karen, it's the best thing that could happen to me."

"Really?" Laura asked, holding her son above water.

"Sure, I *gotta* learn how to swim now, and I can't do it in a pool. That won't help me out there." She pointed to the waves.

Ginger turned up her chin slightly and cocked her head.

"What is it?" Laura asked. "Hear something?"

"Maybe. I don't know. Something above the surf. It's like bees or something."

The women stood in the shallow water that still ran through and around their legs. "I hear it too," Val said.

Karen shook her head. "What are you talking about?"

"Listen!" Ginger said.

Karen searched the wide arc of sand that constituted Knots Landing beach. Almost simultaneously five speeding motorcycles shot into view. The riders skirted the water's edge three hundred yards north of where the women stood, sending up foamy wakes. Blue smoke blasted from their tail pipes and the bone-throbbing rip of the engines grew uncomfortably louder.

"A motorcycle gang?" Val asked.

"Maybe they'll just ride past," Ginger said anxiously. She unconsciously crossed her arms in front of her breasts.

"Maybe we should get the hell out of here, huh, girls?" Karen said.

They didn't have time to start for dry sand. The first bike roared up to them at a dizzying speed, then cut right and spun in the shallow water, nearly throwing its leering rider, a blue-jeaned biker with the word "Music" sewn onto the back of his cracked leather jacket.

A second and third bike joined the first, the three riders circling the frightened group of women, their wheels digging into the soft sand and water.

"Jason!" Laura cried as her son dodged a motorcycle and ran toward her. She picked him up, hugged him, then put him down.

The women quickly moved into a reversed huddle, their shoulders together as they stood facing outward, watching the bikes ride around them. Laura moved Jason within the protective ring.

Karen looked up on the beach. Most sunbathers were busy packing up and leaving—the beach was emptying rapidly. The volleyball game had broken up and the players were standing still, watching the bikers. Karen saw Diana standing there, then located Eric and Michael down the beach, staring at her.

She motioned for them to stay where they were.

"You calling me?" one of the bikers said, noticing her signal.

"No!" Karen said.

One of the riders turned too sharply. His bike slid out from under him and crashed toward the volleyball players, who scattered across the beach.

"Hey, girl!" one of the bikers yelled.

"Don't listen to them," Karen shouted, then glared at him.

Why didn't they just leave them alone?

"Yeah, you!" The biker lifted his hand in an obscene gesture. As he did so his wheel hit a clump of seaweed, sending him sprawling to the sand. As the biker fell he grabbed at Ginger's bottom.

"Hey!" Ginger slapped his arm and staggered out of the man's reach.

The biker rolled into the surf. A wave slapped his bearded face, rousing him, He stood, pulled up his motorcycle and leaned it against its kickstand.

"Let's go. Now!" Karen screamed. "Kids! Go!"

Another biker shut off his engine and straddled his bike, arms crossed on his chest. He looked at the three cycles that continued to circle the women.

Karen noticed that two of the bikers were women—one had long, black hair that streamed in the wind. At first she'd thought it was a long-haired man.

"Get 'em, Mary!" the bearded one commanded.

The black-haired woman leapt off the back of the motocycle and headed straight for Karen.

"No!" Diana cried out. She ran furiously, then reached out and grabbed a handful of the woman's hair. Diana yanked it hard.

Mary's body jerked back. "Let me go, bitch! Let me go!" she hissed, twisting savagely.

"Mary, don't let her walk all over you!" the bearded biker taunted.

As Mary turned, Diana thrust her knee into the woman's stomach, then shoved her face-down into the sand. She sprinted over to her mother.

The bikers had widened their circle and finally broke the formation and rode crazily along the edge of the undulating surf.

"Let's go!" Diana said, clutching her mother's hand.

They joined Ginger, Val, Laura, Jason, Eric and Michael as they frantically gathered up their belongings. Diana glanced furtively over her shoulder at Mary, the female biker. She sat on the sand shaking her head.

"Get up, Mary!" one of the bikers yelled.

She stood and, with a piercing glare at Diana, hopped onto the back of one of the motorcycles.

The group of women and children were moving away when three of the motorcycles pulled up directly before them on the beach.

One biker grinned menacingly and scratched his chin as he stared at Laura.

"You look like a lady who knows how to show a man a good time," he said. "What about it? You and me together?"

"You leave my mother alone!" Jason said, breaking free from his mother's grip. He pounded his seven-year-old fists against the biker's meaty thigh.

"I think my friend Alien here likes you," Music said to Laura.

"Tell your friend I'm not interested," Laura snapped, her face firm, eyes set. She reached for Jason. "Come on, honey," she said and pulled him to her.

The women and children huddled together, still holding towels and baskets, waiting. The bikers moved and blocked their exit from the beach.

"Hey, what's all this hostility here?" Music said. "Bad vibes, man. Why're you beating up my buddy?'' He knelt before Jason.

''Leave my son alone!'' Laura cried, jerking the boy back.

''No one's touching your son. We just wanted to join in the fun,'' Music said, and suddenly caught Karen's gaze. He smiled more broadly. His eyes were mocking, electric—poisonous.

''No one invited you,'' Ginger said.

''It's a free country, right, ladies? God bless America and all that. Huh?''

''That's right, Music.'' Alien nodded.

''Right.'' Karen breathed deeply. ''So get out of our way. We're leaving.''

''Sure,'' Music said. He and the other bikers stepped back.

Diana took her mother's hand as they started toward the ramp that led up to the parking lot. Alien pounced as they moved, landing before Karen.

''Let's you and me have a little talk, Mama.'' The biker eyed her luridly. ''You get me hot.''

Karen's stomach heaved. The thought of touching him revolted her. She thought of her baby and found new strength. *''Leave me alone!''*

Diana stiffened beside her mother as Alien stared at Karen.

Eric jumped in front of her, his young face stern. ''You heard her, mister,'' he ordered. ''She doesn't want to talk to you''

Alien glowered. ''Man, I'm getting tired of bratty kids.'' He set up a punch on the boy's chin.

''Alien, cool it,'' Music warned. ''Just back off. The ladies don't want to play—do you, ladies?''

''No,'' Ginger said.

29

"We'd like to go home." Laura's voice was controlled but tense.

"Fine. Like I said—free country." Music smiled. Once again he and Alien moved back.

The women and children walked en masse toward the ramp. As she walked Karen could feel the men following them. She looked over her shoulder, then quickly forward. "Motorcycles aren't allowed on the beach," she said, loud enough so that the bikers would hear.

"And the lifeguard patrol will be here any minute," Eric added, shifting the beach chair from one hand to another.

Alien ran past the group and stopped before them, eyes gleaming. The wind whipped his shoulder-length hair. "Hey, ladies, that just scares the pants right off me!" With that he unbuttoned and then dropped his jeans—revealing brightly colored boxer shorts.

"I've seen better," Val muttered.

Ginger laughed. Karen stood shocked, uncertain.

Alien, his anger apparently forgotten, turned toward the beach, kicked off his pants and boots, and ran into the surf. The other bikers suddenly lost all interest in the women and children. They went back to their machines and broke out beer, smokes and snacks.

"Come on!" Karen prompted.

They hurried up the ramp.

"Val, you're so brave! If he'd heard you!" Ginger exclaimed.

"He didn't."

"I'm proud of you, honey," Karen said as she tousled Eric's hair. "You too, Diana."

30

"Me too." Laura patted Jason's shoulder.

"I'm just glad it's over," Michael said. "I don't like them."

Karen turned back for a moment and looked at the beach. It was nearly deserted—only Alien, Music, Mary and their friends now occupied it. They'd won.

Karen shook her head. "I hate them! They have no right!"

"Hey, Karen, calm down." Val put her arm around Karen's shoulder. "It's not like they hurt us or anything."

"They could have," she said. "They sure could have," she repeated.

Karen was rigid with fury as they loaded up the cars and headed home to safety.

Richard Avery sat on the Fairgates' sofa opposite Sergeant Wayne Willis. Ginger, Karen, Laura and Val sat around the room and listened as Richard spoke.

"Karen, if you can't provide the police with any concrete information, with something they can work with, I'm afraid that their hands are tied. I couldn't even serve them with a restraining order unless—"

"Nobody had time to write down license plate numbers, Richard!" Karen said.

"It all happened so fast, honey." Laura added.

Ginger sighed. "The license plates are so small— who can see them?"

Sergeant Willis, a bear of a man with an exhausted but sincere face, cleared his throat. "We'll take another look around the area, but unless we actually catch them on the beach I'm afraid there's nothing we can do." He shook his head.

"That's not good enough," Karen insisted. "There *must* be something you can do."

Sid Fairgate strode into the room, Gary Ewing following him.

"How is everybody?" he asked.

"You wouldn't have believed it, Sid! Bikers! Racing through the surf right at us."

"Anybody hurt?" Sid's face darkened with concern.

"Fortunately, no," Ginger answered.

"You okay, honey?" Gary touched his wife's shoulder.

"I'm fine." Val smiled at him.

Richard coughed for silence. "I don't think you'll find them, Sergeant Willis."

"Thanks for your vote of confidence, Mr. Avery." He smiled.

"You know their type—out looking for trouble. They don't care where they have it or who gets hurt while they're doing it. I think they didn't find the trouble they wanted, so they moved on. It'll be San Diego's problem tomorrow."

"I sure hope you're right," Karen said.

"You could be right, but I don't think so," Sergeant Willis said. "We'll keep an eye out."

Richard turned to his wife. "Laura, I don't suppose you had a chance to start dinner, did you?"

"Sorry, honey," Laura apologized. "What with all the confusion and talking to Sergeant Willis, I just didn't—"

"Great," he replied sarcastically.

"Hey, it hasn't exactly been a quiet day at

home!'' Laura exclaimed, her anger rising.

"Yes, and my stomach will be the only casualty.'' He dismissed the matter with an annoyed shake of his head and trailed off toward the door.

Laura gave the others an apologetic look as she got up. She spread out her hands in a helpless gesture, then followed her husband out.

Val and Gary rose. "We should be going too,'' Val said.

"Goodnight, you guys,'' Sid said as they left.

"I sure hope Richard's right,'' Karen sighed when the Ewings had gone. "I can't believe it's over yet, though.''

"We'll do everything we can,'' Willis promised. "I've got to be getting back. See you.'' He tipped his hat and left quickly.

Sid and Karen looked at each other across the deserted living room. "Karen,'' he said. "You okay? You've been acting—well, different.''

"Of course,'' she straightened her shoulders. "I'm not used to dealing with motorcycle gangs.''

"No, it's something more than that,'' Sid coaxed.

Karen looked at him squarely. "What then? What do you mean?''

He shook his head, "I don't know.'' Sid rose and walked off toward the kitchen. "I don't know.''

Karen sat and thought. Somehow Sid does know. He knows I'm pregnant. But how? Does it show on my face, or in my eyes? Have I changed?

She thought of it again after dinner, as she sat on the couch, trying to make sense of it all. But her mind flashed back to the beach that afternoon. Devastating emotions welled up within her. Karen felt herself shake with rage as she remembered the bikers.

Trying to distract herself, she picked up a stack of magazines, rifled through them, and then slapped them on the table. She pushed a chair three inches to the right, then a foot to the left, and then returned it to its original position. She rearranged some pillows on the couch.

Let me think about anything else but them, Karen told herself. She opened a drawer and then slammed it shut in frustration and anger.

The lights suddenly went out. Karen looked up and saw Sid's outline near the light switch on the wall.

"How long—" Karen started, and then sighed.

"You haven't cooled down yet?" Sid said, walking toward her in the darkened room.

"I'm livid."

Sid stroked her arm. "Was it that horrible?" he asked.

Karen shrugged. "You know how I am—I get my nose out of joint when someone smokes in the elevator. Of course I'm mad! Those people rode their motorcycles on the beach and threatened us. Why *shouldn't* I be angry?"

"You were probably the best-looking ones on the beach," Sid kidded lightly.

Karen snapped her head toward him. "Don't you *dare* make jokes about this, Sid! This is serious!"

"Who's making jokes?" He drew her toward him. "I mean it. Really."

Karen moved from him and sat in the

darkness, then relaxed against the seat cushions.

Sid sighed. "I'll go shut off the garage light," he said, and left the room.

Karen rubbed her forehead. Even if we *were* the best-looking ones on the beach that didn't give them the right to terrorize us. Endangering the children was inexcusable. Sid doesn't realize how dangerous it was, Karen brooded.

Children. Baby. Pregnant.

Those thoughts came back to her again. She tried to ignore them but they kept on coming.

Karen looked at the hallway in which Sid had just disappeared. She should tell Sid everything, tonight, so he could understand. Telling him everything wouldn't make her decision any easier, but at least she'd get Sid's input.

She started to walk to the garage and then stopped. No, she couldn't tell him tonight. She wasn't in the mood and couldn't possibly handle his concern and questions.

Karen walked alone to the stairs instead. In the morning, she decided. She'd tell Sid in the morning.

Chapter Three

Turmoil

Dazzling sunshine streamed in through the bedroom windows. Karen Fairgate yawned and opened her eyes, then laid a hand on her stomach uncertainly.

"Hey, anybody in there?" she whispered.

Sid groaned, thrashed in his sleep, then settled quietly down beside her.

Karen sighed, rose from bed without waking her husband, wrapped herself in a soft blue robe and left the room. Walking by Diana's bedroom, Karen stopped abruptly. She heard voices. Diana must be up, but who was with her? She paused, then bent her ear toward the door and listened.

"I'm glad to see you," Diana said, her voice rich and purring, far too seductive to be that of a sixteen-year-old child. "You will be staying, won't you?"

Diana's voice grew more erotic, with a come-on-and-hurry-up quality which Karen found quite realistic—*too* realistic. She knocked.

"Come in," Diana said, in the same voice.

Karen pushed open the door and surveyed the room. Diana sat on her bed, alone, holding a slim book.

"Good morning." Karen looked puzzled. "You're up early."

"I know," Diana said.

"What's up?"

She smiled cheerfully. "I'm auditioning for the school play, so I have to practice. That's one of the lines in the scene we're using, the 'You will be staying . . .' one. I'm supposed to say it real scutzy."

Karen sat on the bed beside her. "Scutzy?"

Her daughter nodded. "Scutzy. It says to do it that way. It's a stage direction."

Karen stifled a yawn. "Where does it say scutzy?" She took the book from her daughter and, running a finger down the two opened pages, found the line. She smiled. "It says 'coquettishly,'" Karen said. "Cookie, coquettish means flirtatious."

"It does?" Diana's face blank. "I thought it meant . . ."

"Yeah, I guess, the way you were doing it."

"Yeah. Oh well, coquettish is easy." Diana closed the book and grinned.

Karen kissed her daughter's forehead, then smoothed back her hair. "You and the boys, the way you stuck up for me. I was proud of you."

"It was nothing," Diana said. "If someone had come after one of us—I'd sure feel sorry for them! One for all and all for one, right?" Her voice was crisp with confidence.

Karen smiled, then nodded. "You're right,

cookie. I just hope it never happens again." Karen rose. "When did you suddenly get interested in drama?"

"I didn't *suddenly*. It happened a few weeks ago. Buzzy Marek is sure to get the boy's lead."

Karen nodded knowingly. "Ah."

"I'm glad to see you," Diana repeated in a sexy murmur, her voice emanating from behind the door as Karen closed it. "You will be staying, won't you?"

Karen turned toward the stairs, then with determination went back to the bedroom. Sid was sitting up, rubbing his stubbly face with both hands.

"Sid, let's talk," she said.

"Sure." He pounded the bed beside him. "Close the door and come back to bed. I'll give you some conversation." He chuckled.

"Okay." She slipped off the robe, threw it over the edge of the bed, then slid in beside him. "Cuddle me," she said, and snuggled next to her husband.

They lay side by side, Sid's arm wrapped around Karen's body. She could feel his heartbeat: strong, confident, manly.

"Sid, we have to talk."

"Sure, sweetheart." He kissed her ear.

"I'm serious."

Sid sighed. "Okay."

"It isn't easy to bring it up." Karen's mouth was tense and dry. "But here goes. Yesterday, after I found out . . ."

"Found out what, darling?" Sid's voice reverberated through the room. "You don't mean those bikers on the beach, do you?" he

38

added in a worried tone.

"Let me tell it my way, okay?" Karen spoke softly, careful not to raise her voice.

"Of course. Sorry." He nuzzled her neck.

"For a while, every other possible thought crossed my mind, every other plausible explanation. It was so unexpected that I hadn't had any real time to prepare for it. My head's been a jumble since yesterday morning."

"Don't I know that!" Sid said. "Even the kids mentioned it. Are you sick or something?"

Karen shook her head. "Sid, please . . ." she said imploringly.

"Sorry."

"I'm thirty-seven years old, and I know who I am. That's no small thing knowing that, Sid. A lot of people have no idea who they are. I also like what I do, and I'm good at it. I'm happy with my family and friends, and I live in a beautiful house on Seaview Circle." She paused a moment.

Sid didn't break in. He sat watching her, expectantly.

She sat up and turned to him. "Sid, I'm pregnant." The words came out in a rush. Karen locked her eyes on his, biting her lower lip, waiting for his reaction.

"Karen!" Sid sat up, his lower jaw suspended. "Really?" he asked, after a few seconds.

"Yes." Karen pushed back from him. "I am. It's definite. I've had the test and everything."

"But—" Sid said, his face melting from astonishment. "I can't believe it!"

"Tell me what you're thinking—right now." Karen's face was still set with tension.

"I'm thinking that you're pregnant!" he said.

"How do you feel about that? Tell me honestly, Sid," she pleaded. "I need to know."

He started to answer, then stood up and paced. Karen lay down on her side of the bed, her head propped up with one hand.

Sid shook his head. "I guess I don't know how I feel—because I don't know how *you* feel about it."

Karen sat up. "But when I first said it—Sid, I'm pregnant—what did you think then?"

"Honestly?" Sid's hands rested on his hipbones.

Karen briefly closed her eyes. "Please."

"I thought, my God, we're going to have a baby!" Sid smiled broadly.

Karen was silent, eyes downcast.

"What's wrong, Karen?" he asked, and gazed at her.

She looked up at him, her face grim, and bit her lower lip. Sid's face darkened

"We *are* going to have a baby, aren't we?"

Karen collapsed onto her back and stared at the ceiling. "I don't know, Sid. I just don't know."

He sat beside her, pressing his fingers to his forehead. "I see," he said.

"I just don't think I can make a decision about this right now, with all the trouble on the beach."

"Hey, that's over," Sid said. "Don't worry about that. Just keep your mind on matters at hand."

Karen laughed bitterly. "Do you think I've been able to think about anything else?" She was quiet for a moment. "I just wanted to know how you felt about it."

Sid searched her eyes for more information as

he stood beside the bed, but found none.

Downstairs, an hour later, Diana, Michael and Eric made breakfast for themselves.

"You know what?" Michael said as he took a carton of milk from the refrigerator.

"I don't care," Diana teased him.

"I'm serious," Michael implored. "It's about Mom."

"So?" Eric said, sitting at the table.

"So . . . something's wrong with her." Michael's face was drawn with worry.

"It was that gang on the beach yesterday," Diana said.

"No it's not! She was like that before we went to the beach. Don't you remember?"

"That's right," Eric agreed. "And we don't need you to tell us that. Remember when Mom asked me to back the car out of the driveway, and I had to tell her, 'Mom, I don't drive'?"

"It's probably some female thing—but I don't know which one," Diana said with authority.

Michael and Eric lifted their shoulders, defeated in the face of unknown territory.

Meanwhile, Sid, upstairs, was slipping on an undershirt. "How're you feeling now?"

"I don't know," Karen answered. "Fine. Wonderful. Great. Miserable!" Karen languished in bed.

"I know," Sid sympathized. "I can imagine how you feel."

"I'm totally rattled, Sid. I mean, how can I make a decision about something like this? Before, when I was younger, there wasn't any question—no problem at all. The last sixteen years of my life have been spent with diapers and pacifiers, scraped knees and runny noses . . . as well as birthdays and Christmas days and little presents that made it so wonderful.'' She scowled. ''*That's* what's so maddening now!''

''Honey, there's no rush on this,'' Sid began.

''Oh yes there is!'' she cried. ''What am I supposed to do, just forget I'm pregnant until I decide what to do about it? There's a human being growing inside me!'' She placed her hands on her slim stomach.

Sid answered her with silence.

''I've paid my dues, Sid,'' she continued, shaking her head. ''I've done it three times now. I don't know whether I can do it again. I'm only human.'' She turned to him beseechingly. ''Don't just stand there, Sid! What do you think?''

''I think it's your decision,'' he said, his voice neutral.

''Fine! I'll decide, but what do you think?''

Sid's gaze dropped to the floor. ''I think you should have the baby,'' he said quietly.

Karen's face reddened. ''Of course you do!'' she said, spitting her words. ''It's so easy to say that! You ought to try having a baby sometime.''

''Oh, come on, sweetheart!'' Sid was exasperated. ''You just asked me what I thought, and I told you. You don't have to explode just because I do what you tell me.''

Diana walked into their bedroom. ''What are you guys yelling about up here?'' she asked.

They both turned, surprised to see Diana standing in the doorway.

''Who's having a baby?'' Diana asked slowly.

''I'm pregnant, Diana,'' Karen replied, rising

from the bed and nervously smoothing her gown.

Diana gasped. "You're what?"

"I'm pregnant. Believe me, it's true."

"But you can't be pregnant!" Diana exclaimed in utter disbelief.

"She is, honey. That's what she's trying to tell you." Sid smiled briefly at his daughter.

"But why?" Diana stared at her mother.

Karen looked at Sid and smirked. "It used to be that *how* was the hardest question to answer. This is tougher." She turned back to Diana. "It wasn't planned."

"Another baby?" Diana went on. "Mother, how *could* you?"

"Look, Diana," Karen said, with mounting impatience.

"It's hard enough as it is. Don't make things any worse, okay, sweetie?" Sid added.

Diana continued to stare at her mother, and then, abruptly, stormed out of the room.

Karen uneasily watched her go. A moment later she slumped back down on the pillow.

Sid turned to look at her in eloquent silence.

Downstairs at the breakfast table Diana broke into her brothers' conversation.

"Leave some for me." She grabbed the cereal box from Michael's hand.

"Some what?" Michael asked.

"What's wrong with you?" Eric stared at his sister's strange expression.

"You're mad because your face broke out again?" Michael asked.

Diana flashed him a look of death. "You want to know what's happening right here, in our house, under our noses?"

43

"What?" Eric asked.

"Mom's pregnant."

The boys looked at her in shock.

"Oh, come on." Eric laughed.

"She's too old." Michael laughed too.

Diana shook her head. "Wrong! She's too old to start raising a new baby, maybe, but she's not too old to be pregnant."

Michael and Eric looked at each other, exchanging confusion and amazement.

Karen walked into the kitchen swiftly, then slowed as she summed up the situation. Her sons turned toward her, and Diana glanced at her mother. There was a moment of panicked silence and embarrassment.

"Well, since you all know anyway," Karen said to the boys, "it looks like we'd better have a little talk." She sat at the table. As Karen was about to speak again someone tapped on the patio door.

"Hi, everyone." Valene Ewing stuck her head in through the doorway.

"Hi, Val," Karen said. "Come on in."

Val walked into the kitchen. As she approached them, Michael turned to her.

"Mrs. Ewing, my mom's pregnant!" he blurted out.

Karen sighed and threw her hands down.

"Karen!" Val looked stunned. Her eyes lit up. "Is it true?"

"Yep," she said matter-of-factly. "I heard it yesterday at Dr. Bender's."

"So Ginger was right! Something *was* up with you." Val ran across the room and hugged Karen. "I can't believe it!"

"That makes two of us," Karen nodded, lamely accepting the embrace.

"Three," Diana added and turned from the room.

Val straightened up and leaned against the table. "What's wrong with her?" she asked.

Karen smiled. "She didn't take the news well."

"Boy, I'll say!" Michael spouted.

"I think you've said enough for the time being, young man," Karen said. "Finish your breakfast and get ready for school. Both of you."

An hour later, after Karen did some fast phoning, Laura Avery stopped by the Fairgate house, joining Karen, Ginger and Val. They were all sipping iced tea in the living room and gossiping.

Ginger turned to Karen after Laura was settled in. "You're so calm about this whole thing, Karen," she said. "I'd be a bundle of nerves."

"Maybe I look calm on the outside," Karen said quietly.

"You and Sid weren't planning this, were you?"

"No, Laura. It was quite a surprise."

"Even so, you must be excited," Valene said, and then giggled. "I remember—" she began, then grew silent.

"How *does it* feel, Karen?" Ginger asked.

Karen studied herself for a moment. "If you want to know the truth, I'm confused. A part of me is changing already. I feel kind of, well, full of life— it's a good feeling, I'll admit!"

"It sure is," Laura added. "It's different from anything else I ever experienced in my whole life."

45

"It's hard to fight those old maternal instincts," Karen said grudgingly.

"I don't understand," Ginger inquired sweetly. "Then why fight them?"

"Because there's another part of me, a big part, that's screaming 'Wait a minute! I've had three kids, I've paid my dues to motherhood, and now it's time for *me*—.'"

"But being a mother!" Val interrupted. "That's more special than anything I can think of."

"I think so, too," Ginger said. "I'm so envious of you, Karen. And happy for you." She noticed the clock. "I've got to get to school. Think of me at the beach this afternoon!" She waved and left.

"What about Sid and the kids?" Laura asked.

"Yeah. How does Sid feel about this?" Val echoed.

Karen shrugged. "I don't know. The kids are confused. Diana seems upset—maybe more than she should be. I don't know. I can't expect them to be anything but confused."

Val leaned forward on the couch. "Karen, you aren't—I mean, you're not thinking of having . . ."

Karen stopped her. "I don't know. Right now, I don't know anything, except that I am definitely pregnant."

The other women nodded silently. There was really nothing more to say.

As Sid tinkered under the hood of his car that afternoon, Gary Ewing stopped by.

"It's been kinda rough on Karen these last few days, hasn't it?" Gary said handing him a larger wrench and leaning against the car.

Sid wiped the sweat from his forehead onto the sleeve of his stained coveralls. "You could say that."

"I mean, the pregnancy, the bikers on the beach. That's more than any woman should have to go through at the same time."

"Well, Richard's probably right—we won't have to worry about the bikers again. That gang must have moved on by now."

"I *hope* he's right, Sid, but I'm not betting on it." He frowned. "I don't think we should let the women go to the beach again today."

"I'm sure they'll be fine," Sid said, then banged his finger. "Damn!"

Gary coughed. "I thought about bringing over cigars, but I guess *you're* supposed to do that. And champagne's not my thing," he said with a slight smile.

Sid lifted his head from the car's guts. "Don't worry about it. It's still too early to celebrate."

"That's right," Gary said. "You've got seven months to go."

"Maybe not," Sid mused, shaking his head. He wiped his hands on a rag.

"What are you talking about, maybe not?"

"Karen might not have the baby."

"What, is something wrong? Is she sick?"

Sid grunted. "No, nothing like that. She's— Karen isn't sure it's what she wants."

Gary raised his eyebrows. "What do you think about that?"

"I want what's best for Karen," Sid said evenly.

"Sid, you can't mean that!"

"All right, I want her to have the baby," he confessed.

"You had me worried for a minute there," Gary said with relief.

"Sure I want her to have it. When she told me I felt terrific, but ever since then I've felt guilty for feeling so good."

"Why?"

"Because Karen might not want the baby. Hell, I know it's my baby too, but it's not the same thing. I don't have to *have* it. After it's born I'll keep going to work, coming home to it for an hour of play, enjoying it without investing any real time in it. I won't have to nurse the kid, change its diapers, or raise it day in day out. I want that baby, Gary, but I want what Karen wants more."

Gary nodded. "So what are you going to do?"

"Trust Karen," Sid said, "It's all I can do." He stuck his head back into the guts of his cherry red classic Chevy.

Karen pulled her station wagon into the beach parking lot. From it emerged Val, Laura, Diana and Michael, as well as Karen. Below them the water sparkled an inviting blue. Before removing the beach equipment from the car, Karen walked to the ramp and peered down at the beach.

"No sign of the bikers," she called back. "Looks like the beach is safe for democracy."

Michael and the women looked at each other, relieved but not surprised. They unloaded their beach paraphernalia and started down the long, steep ramp that led to the beach.

"If it's safe for democracy, that means I've got

a right not to get wet if I don't want to," Val stated while struggling with a cooler.

"Are you chickening out again, Val?" Karen goaded.

"I'm thinking about it."

"Why isn't Ginger here today?" Diana asked.

"She had to take her class on a field trip," Laura said.

They went halfway down the sand toward the water. "This looks like a good spot." Laura dropped the blankets and towels.

"Field trips in kindergarten?" Val questioned.

"Ginger's very progressive," Laura answered.

As they settled in, Val looked to the edge of the water, then followed the sweep of the beach to each side. "Oh no," she said slowly.

The others turned their heads. The whine of engines was already discernible even before the cycles burst into view from the opposite direction that they had come from last time. The bikers barrelled down the beach toward the women.

"Not again!" Karen shouted. "I knew it."

Her words were lost in the roar of the motorcycles. The five bikers pulled up ten feet from the women and stopped. Karen noticed that the female bikers weren't present.

Val gripped Karen's hand as the men sat gunning their bikes. Alien, the bearded man, grinned.

"Well, look who's back!" he said. "Didn't expect to see you here." Alien turned back to the gang. "Let's give it to 'em!"

The bikers scattered around the terrified group.

"Oh, my God!" Karen cried.

Music waved as he sped past her. The motorcycles moved in short spurts across the beach, their front wheels digging into the sand. It made them more menacing, Karen thought, as she squeezed Val's hand.

"Don't move, Diana, Michael," Karen warned. "Let's just wait this out."

"Okay, Mom," Michael said quietly as he turned toward her.

Who the hell do these bikers think they are? Karen straightened her shoulders and exhaled forcefully.

"Ladies!" Alien called, driving by again.

The five machines started zig-zagging across the beach, disrupting nearly everyone on it. No one seemed to be hurt, Karen noticed, but once again the beach was emptying quickly.

"Get out of here! Just leave us alone!" Valene screamed. As one of the bikes passed too close to her, Val hit out at the man's face. He laughed. "Do it some more!" he yelled.

Alien circled past Karen again. When he was within reach the biker grabbed the shirttails of Karen's blouse, which she hadn't yet removed.

"Let my mother go!" Michael screeched, rushing forward. The boy pulled the shirt and yanked it from Alien's hands.

"Damn it!" Alien snapped. His front wheel hit a deep hole in the sand, and his motorcycle tilted suddenly to the right. His handlebars twisted as he struggled to escape from the hole. As they went through their gyrations the handlebars struck Michael's forehead squarely, knocking him to the ground backwards.

"Michael!" Karen cried, stung into action. She

ran to him. "Michael, honey, are you okay?" She ignored the sand spraying over her from the wheels of the still circling bikes. "Scum!" she shouted to Alien, brushing sand from her son's face.

"Look!" Laura said.

Two policemen hurried down the ramp toward the beach.

"The cops!" Diana shouted.

"Come on, let's split!" Alien gunned his bike and the gang broke into two groups, then disappeared down the beach in both directions.

Karen knelt over her son, touching the blood seeping from his forehead, as the sound of the engines mixed with the roar of the ocean and eventually died out.

Chapter Four

Lock Up

Sid Fairgate snapped the steering wheel to the left as he drove into the hospital parking lot, the car's jolting movements punctuating his anger. He saw Karen pacing outside the emergency room entrance.

If I ever get my hands on those creeps, Sid seethed, his lips pulled tight. I never should have let them go to the beach.

Sid slipped into a narrow space marked "No Parking" next to a CAT-scan trailer. "Karen!" he called, running to the steps where she stood.

"How is he?" Sid asked as he puffed up to her.

"He's okay," Karen answered, arms crossed tight against her chest. Her face was set, angry; her eyes slick.

"I came as fast as I could," Sid said.

"They're stitching him up now." She shuddered. "I couldn't stand being in there any longer."

"Any concussion or anything?"

"No." Karen shook her head. "Thankfully, no." She turned to look through the emergency room's glass door.

"Honey, are you okay?" Sid caressed her hair lightly.

"I'm fine." She didn't look at him but pulled tighter on her shoulders with her hands. "Really, Sid, I'm fine."

"Was Sergeant Willis here? Did you talk to him yet?"

"Sure." Karen's word hung for a moment. "He was here. They're supposed to be out looking for them right now." She frowned.

"Karen," Sid said. "I'm sure they're doing the best—"

"Michael!" Karen pushed in through the door after seeing her son being escorted into the room by a doctor. Michael's head was wrapped in unnaturally white bandages.

"Oh no!" Karen's eyes filled with tears.

"Looks worse than it really is," the man reassured her. "I'm Doctor Bucher." He pulled on the ends of his beard. "Had to give him six stitches."

"That's not all." Michael grimaced.

"That's right," the doctor said. "Your son has some kind of haircut under there."

"Dr. Bucher, I'm Michael's father. How is he?"

The man smiled. "Come back in a week and I'll take the stitches out." He patted Michael's shoulder. "Got to get back to work. You be careful," he said to Michael.

"I will."

"We'll make sure he will," Karen said.

"Thank you, Dr. Bucher." She gently touched the edge of Michael's bandage.

"Yes, thank you," Sid threw in. Then he whispered in Karen's ear, "Don't we have to pay him?"

Karen nudged him away. "I used the insurance card. Let's get home." She stroked her son's cheek. "You really okay?"

"Sure, Mom," Michael said, then screwed up his face. "It's all those drugs they gave me."

"Not funny, young man." Karen tried to be stern.

"Does it hurt, Michael?" Sid asked.

He shook his head slightly. "Not yet. It might when the anaesthetic wears off."

"Well, thank God, you're okay! Karen, where's your car?"

"I sent Laura and the others home in it. I wasn't going anywhere anyway." Karen's face was grim.

"I just can't believe I let you go," Sid said as they stopped before his car.

He drove in silence for four blocks as Karen sat looking out the side window, her elbow bent, hand supporting her chin. Their son finally interrupted their thoughts.

"Boy, I'm not too crazy about growing up," the twelve-year-old said.

"Why's that, sport?" his father asked.

Michael frowned. "The last time I had to have stitches I got a lollipop." He sighed. "I could sure use one right now. I'd even eat a green one."

Sid laughed and turned to Karen, who showed no signs of having heard them. He exchanged a worried glance with Michael through the rear view mirror.

"I hate this feeling," Karen said, not turning from the side window.

"What feeling?" Sid asked.

"This feeling of, well, helplessness. I had to stand there and watch that man split open my son's head. I had no control over what he did or who he hurt. I feel like I've been . . . it's like being touched when you don't want to be, by something you don't want to touch you. I don't know." She shook her head.

The swells of passing cars filled the silence for a few moments.

"Karen, there's no reason to do this to yourself," Sid said, keeping his eyes on the road. Michael was now dozing, open-mouthed.

"Do what?" she asked.

"You know. Let the police handle it."

Karen smirked. "The police? What can they do? They can't get a few people off the beach!"

"Yes," Sid said. "They're up against a lot."

"That's not good enough!" Karen's whisper was harsh.

"Okay, okay, Forget I ever mentioned it."

They rode in silence.

A few minutes later, Michael awoke. "Hey look!" he exclaimed, sitting up suddenly. "There, up ahead! It's them, Mom. It's *them*!" Michael pointed toward a fast-food restaurant. Next to the back of the building, beside the restrooms, sat two motorcycles. Music and Alien stood beside them.

"My God, it *is* them!" Karen cringed. "I can't

believe they're still in town. Slow down, Sid, please slow down!"

"You mean those guys?" Sid stared at the two unsavory men. He pulled over to the curb fifty feet from the restaurant. The bikers had their backs turned to them.. Sid glanced at Karen. "Stay here," he said firmly. "I'll take care of them."

"What are you going to do to them—alone?" Karen's eyes were sharp with fear.

"Just stay here! You too, Michael!"

Sid shut the door quietly, then approached the restaurant. He walked slowly, deliberately, controlling his rage, channelling it into his defense systems. The door to the men's room lay open, and the biker with "Music" on his jacket stood leaning against the edge of the door as he dragged off a cigarette.

"Excuse me," Sid said. "Can I bum a smoke from one of you guys?"

"Sure," Music said, without looking up.

Alien swung around and took in Sid. "That's him! That's the kid's father—I saw him at the house when I rode by last night."

Sid rammed his foot into Music's midsection. The biker stumbled backward into the restroom, banged against the grimy tiled wall, and slumped to a squat.

"You!" Alien started.

Sid powered a punch into the man' stomach. Alien doubled over long enough for Sid to swing the man around and grip his right arm. Sid twisted it savagely against Alien's back, kicked the men's room door shut, then slammed Alien against it, trapping Music inside.

"Hey, man!" Music said in a muffled voice while Sid struggled with Alien. "Let me outa here!"

"Listen, punk," Sid hissed, his mouth inches from Alien's sweating ear. "I ought to break your neck for what you did to my son." Sid jerked the arm even higher.

Alien howled in pain. "Let me go!"

Music pounded on the door, sending shock waves through Alien's body as Sid tightened his grip.

"Sid!" Karen shouted somewhere behind him.

"Karen, call the cops!"

"Right!"

Sid looked over his shoulder and saw his wife run to the phone booth in the corner of the parking lot.

"Hey, man, you're hurting me," Alien complained with a whine. "I ain't done nothin' to you. Come on, let me go!" His sinewy body thrashed against the door but Sid held the arm firmly with just enough pressure. If Alien suddenly jerked it the bones would snap.

"Come on, man." Music banged on the door again. "Cut the game!"

"The game's over, punk!" Sid yelled.

Karen stumbled up to him. "They're on the way," she said, her voice breathy. As she turned to face Alien, Karen steeled herself visibly. Her back arched, her eyelids closed slightly and trembled. She put her clasped hands against her mid-section.

Alien sneered at her from his contorted position. "You want something, lady?"

She nodded, balled her hands into fists, and held them straight down beside her. "Yeah, I want something. But this'll have to do." Karen strode to the motorcycles that stood next to each other. She put her hands on her hips and kicked her foot against the closest motorcycle.

"No!" Alien roared.

The machine tilted, striking the other bike. Metallic scrapes rang out as the two bikes hit the ground with a palpable impact. A headlight shattered.

"I'll get you for that, lady!" Alien screamed.

"Hey, let me out of here, damn it!" Music pounded on the door.

"I hate you," Karen glowered at Alien. "You made a big mistake when you hurt my son."

"Hey, it was an accident," Alien said. "You know that. Just havin' some fun on the sand."

A police car rolled into the parking lot. Sid glanced at it and smiled. Alien twisted in his hands but Sid tightened his grip. "You're not going anywhere, buddy," he snarled.

"Come on, man. I'll pay you, anything! Just don't let them lock me up! I can't stand that!"

Sergeant Willis walked up with a uniformed officer. "Hello, Sid, Karen," he said, twirling a pair of handcuffs on one finger. Sid held Alien still as Willis snapped the cuffs around his wrists.

"Damn!" the biker spat.

Willis took him to his car, then placed him in the back seat.

"You know, the guy in the bathroom is awfully quiet," Sid said to Karen, then turned to Willis. "I've got another one in the men's room."

"Looks like I got here just in time," Willis said.

"Two against one?"

"I had things under control," Sid said with pride.

"You sure did, sweetie." Karen smiled.

Sid opened the men's room door, reached in, and yanked Music out by his jacket collar.

Willis whistled. "Not bad, Sid. Didn't know you had it in you." He took Music by the neck of his jacket.

"Oh Sid, stop showing off." Karen laughed.

"You'll file a complaint, then?" Willis asked Karen.

"I'll file fifty if you'd like." She took Sid's hand in hers.

"What about him?" Willis said, and shook Music, who stood passively in the man's grip.

"Hey, don't damage the goods," the biker grumbled.

Karen stood staring at Music. "Well, he wasn't on the bike that hit Michael, and he never touched any of us." Her face was uncertain.

"I could make him a little uncomfortable on a disturbing the peace charge," Willis suggested.

"Come on, man!" Music said. "Let me go." He looked at Karen. "Remember me? I'm your friend!"

Karen hesitated. "That's a lie . . . Still, he was the only one who seemed half-human." Her mouth turned down. "I guess I couldn't really accuse him of anything."

"Okay." He released Music.

The biker stood there, rubbing his neck.

"Can you two come down to the station house now?" Willis asked. "You know, paper work."

"We'll follow you," Karen said. Willis got into

his patrol car and waited at the parking lot exit.

Music stood in front of Karen. "This isn't the end, you know," he said in a sinister whisper. "You haven't won." He turned toward his motorcycle and grimaced. "Damn! What happened to my bike?" He ran to it and bent over, then struggled to upright it.

"Let's go," Karen's expression was a mixture of satisfaction and fear.

Michael ran up. "Wow! Dad, that was great!" His voice rang with admiration. "I couldn't see everything, but you were great! Pow!"

"No sweat," Sid said, and wiped his slick forehead.

"Hey Sid." Karen's voice was soft.

"What?"

"Come here." She smiled, and slid up against him, taking his face gently in her hands, pressing her lips to his. Sid answered, holding her to him, his embrace tight, and tighter still.

Karen finally broke the kiss. "Let's go, Duke," she murmured. Sid sighed with pleasure and loosened his arms reluctantly. He looked back at Music, who was still struggling with his motorcycle.

The biker saw Sid's glance and snarled, "I'll get you for this!" The cords of his neck bulged as he strained under the weight of his bike.

"You shouldn't have made me stay in the car," Michael complained. "I missed everything."

"Yes, you did." Karen grinned as Sid unlocked the door for her.

A half hour later, Kenny Ward stood in the Fairgate living room, leaning over, inspecting Michael's bandage.

"What shape is it?" Kenny asked.

"A 'Z,' I think," Michael said. He turned up to stare at the other people circled around him—his family, the Averys, and the Wards. "What am I, a three-ring circus?" Michael looked pleased.

"He seems to be taking it well," Laura observed.

"Very." Karen smiled.

"If it's a 'Z,' you're lucky," Eric commented. "It'll be like Zorro got you."

"Yeah . . . I hope it scars," Michael said.

"Those creeps were a long way from Zorro." Laura shivered.

"Hey, how bad could they have been?" Kenny Ward joked. "They're just a bunch of fun-lovin' guys on a mad romp, that's all."

"Those fun-lovin' guys hurt my son," Karen retorted tightly.

"And their fun-lovin' hands romped all over your wife's body," Laura added.

"Really?" Kenny turned to Ginger. "But I thought you said you *didn't* like them!"

"I wouldn't say all over," Ginger mumbled, ignoring her husband.

"I think Michael should go to bed," Karen said. "Thanks for coming over, but he's fine."

"Hell, always like to pay tribute to a hero," Kenny lightly punched Sid's shoulder. "That was good work you did—catching that biker."

"Sure. Keeps me in shape for the tough fights." Sid threw a punch in the air.

Kenny and Ginger said their good-byes as they left the living room, followed by the Averys.

Closing the door, Sid turned back to look at his wife and sons. "Well, that's that. No more bikers, no more Alien, no more trouble."

"I wish I could be sure of that," Karen said, running her hand across her forehead. "You heard what Music said—it isn't over. Why do I believe him?"

Diana bounded down the stairs holding her script. "Hi, Mom. Can you take me to the audition now? They're casting the boy's lead."

"Sure, cookie," Karen said.

"I can take her if you want, sweetheart."

"No, Sid, it's okay. Some fresh air might clear my head." Karen pecked Sid's cheek and headed for the door beside her bubbly daughter.

"The kids'll drive me home afterward," Diana said.

"Okay. Be careful!" Sid warned her.

The cool night air was invigorating after the closeness of the crowded living room and the tortures of the day. Karen took a deep breath.

"Oh, I almost forgot," Diana said. She raced back inside the house.

Karen moved to the door to watch her daughter. Diana bent and gently kissed Michael beside his bandage. "My brother, the hero. Thanks!"

Michael's face reddened as Diana ran out and closed the door behind her.

"Mom?" Diana said, as her mother backed the car out of the driveway.

"Yes?"

"Now that the one biker is locked up, will the other ones leave us and the beach alone?"

"I don't know." Her mother sighed. "I wish I could tell you, but I don't know."

"What do your instincts tell you?" Diana

asked, thumbing through the script.

Karen narrowed her eyes. "My instincts tell me—" She paused. "That it isn't over yet."

Diana nodded. "Yeah, I had the same kind of feeling too."

They drove in heavy silence to the school.

After dropping off Diana, Karen drove home as quickly as the speed limit would allow. She wanted to clear her mind so she turned on the radio and tried to listen to the music. But nothing seemed to distract her. Frustrated, she switched off the radio and disconcertedly rolled down the window.

I feel unsafe, exposed, Karen thought as she waited at a stoplight. As she sat there a motorcycle pulled up beside her. Karen turned toward it, terrified.

A white-haired grandmother, wrapped in a warm woolen jacket, reknotted the scarf under her chin, then gunned the bike as the light changed.

Karen laughed out loud. There were lots of motorcycles on the road. Only a few belonged to men like Alien and Music. She'd have to train herself not to jump when she heard *that sound*.

Karen pulled into the cul-de-sac, crossed it, and steered up their driveway. Relieved to be home she got out of the car and walked toward the house.

Halfway up the walk, however, she stopped. Someone was there, in the shadows, next to the house.

"Hello?" she said tentatively.

The shadow undulated again, then a bush rustled as someone passed behind it.

Karen shook her head and moved toward the house. If she could just make it inside she'd be fine. Her throat tightened and she didn't breathe as she walked up to the front door.

Five feet from the door a tall figure shot out before her, cutting off her means of escape.

Karen stepped back in surprise and terror, and nearly screamed until she saw the figure's face. It was Music.

"What the hell are you doing here?" Karen asked in a shrill voice. "Get out or I'll call the police!"

"Mrs. Fairgate," he began.

"I'm serious. Don't think that phony charm of yours is going to work on me. It won't! Now get out of here or you'll join your friend!"

"Hey, man, just a minute," he protested, moving slightly toward her.

"I'm not a *man*."

"I only want to talk to you," Music said. He held up his hands. "See? No guns, no knives. I just wanna talk."

"Not to me. Get out of my way." Karen spat the words.

The biker shrugged, then moved to his right. Karen walked up to the door, aware of the man behind her. She unlocked it and pushed the door open. "Sid!" she screamed inside, then turned back to Music.

"I'm warning you—you have no business here."

Sid appeared behind Karen. "What the hell do you want?" Sid gripped Karen's shoulders protectively. "You better have a damned good reason for being here. Maybe I should just call

Sergeant Willis and have him take you away," he threatened.

"Hey, all I wanna do is talk," Music repeated, looking behind Karen and Sid into the house.

"I'm calling the police." Karen moved from her husband's hands.

"No, wait a minute," Sid said. "Let the man talk. If he doesn't say anything, call them." He turned back to Music. "So talk!"

"Great. Look, I only got one thing to say to you people, or to *you*." He stared at Karen. "Drop the charge against Alien."

"Not a chance!" Karen turned to walk inside the house.

"Hey, listen!" Music went on. "I know you're mad. I can't blame you for that—Alien did a stupid thing. He sure had it coming." He pulled a pack of Marlboros from his jacket.

"Don't smoke here," Karen said.

"Okay, okay. Bad vibes," he mumbled, and stuffed the smokes back into his pocket.

"Just get on with it," Sid said.

"Okay. The only thing is, the guys we ride with aren't going nowheres without Alien. They want him back. So, if you drop the charge and they let Alien out of jail, we'll all be on our way and we'll leave you alone."

Karen folded her arms. "And if I don't?"

Music flashed a grin. "Hell, there's no tellin'. These guys are pretty rough. I don't know what kind of horsin' around they'll be up to if they have to wait."

"I'm calling the police," Karen said flatly. "That sounded like a threat to me."

"Finish what you have to say," Sid said,

overruling her. "But make it fast."

"I *am* finished, man. Drop the charges, we split . . . all of us. Otherwise we'll hang around here. We're supposed to hook up with the rest of our guys down at Laguna. If we don't show, they're gonna come lookin' for us. Some of these guys make Alien look like a Sunday school teacher." He smiled brightly for a moment. "Don't say I didn't warn you."

"Sid!" Karen entreated. "Get him out of here!"

The biker moved back into the shadows, where he had evidently hidden his motorcycle.

Sid ushered Karen into the house, then closed and locked the door.

"That sounded like a threat, didn't it?" Karen's voice was hushed and flat, the muscles of her jaw knotted.

"Yeah, I guess it did."

Chapter Five

Eye of the Storm

"Now that's settled, we can start thinking about the baby again—not that it's ever left my mind," Sid said to his wife as they sat together in their dimly lit living room.

Karen shook her head. "I don't believe it. This is no time to relax! Nothing's settled. You just agreed that Music is still threatening us!"

Sid shrugged. "Honey, that—"

"I know what I heard."

"That's just rough-guy talk." Sid rubbed her shoulder. "I'm not worried."

"I *am*."

"Try to calm down, honey." Sid continued to massage her upper back. "You feel so good."

"Do I feel pregnant?" Karen asked flatly.

Sid's hand stopped rotating momentarily, then slowly moved again. "I don't know about that. You just feel good." He pushed up her sleeve and kissed the bare skin of her wrist. "Mmmmm."

Karen moved over on the couch. "Not now, Sid. I don't feel very romantic."

Sid shrugged and removed his hand. "Well . . . okay," he said, and sat sullenly.

"Sorry. I'm just so worried." Karen frowned.

"No need to apologize. I understand." He paused a moment. "So who's this Buzzy Marek that Diana's always talking about?"

"Oh. He's probably going to be cast in this play. Diana likes him, so she's trying to be cast opposite his part."

"This Buzzy must be some guy. I thought Diana hated the theater."

She sighed. "I'm just glad she's taken an interest in drama, no matter what the reason. Besides, from what Diana's told me about the boy, Buzzy Marek does sound like *some guy*."

"You know, Karen? It's just hitting me, these last few days."

"What?"

His eyes were pensive. "I walked into our bathroom the other day, and caught Eric splashing my aftershave all over his cheeks. My aftershave! The boy's only fourteen! But he's growing up. They all are."

"They sure are." Her voice was noncomittal.

"Diana's sixteen. Hell, she could be married and starting a family within a few years. That's— almost *scary*."

"I know. That's what I've been thinking about—in between fits of rage over those bikers." She shook her head. "Imagine—Diana a mother."

"Don't say that," Sid shuddered. "Don't even *think* that. I'm not ready to be called Granddad yet," he insisted, grimacing.

"What do you think about this goo-goo, ga-ga?" Karen patted her belly.

He paused. "I think it's a wonderful idea, Karen." Sid touched her hand. "For some reason I don't think we should pass this up. It's like a—a—"

"What? A sign?" Karen's voice was sarcastic, but searching.

"Hell, I don't know, sweetheart! It seems like there's got to be a reason for this happening now like it is."

Karen rolled her eyes. "Sure, there's a reason. It's called nothing's one-hundred percent. No form of birth control always works."

"That can be easy to forget," Sid said.

"I'll never forget again."

"But despite what I think," he said, stroking her palm, "I just want you to be happy. We all want that, me and the kids. That's the important thing."

"Sid, don't you understand? There's so much more to that."

"What?" he asked.

"There's other things to be taken into consideration. First of all, having the baby may make me happy *now*, but how can I be sure I won't be tearing my hair out within a year?"

Sid smiled. "I can't imagine you doing that."

She ignored him. "And besides that, there's my career, my life, my whole future." She pressed her temples with tense fingers. "I can't just say yes or no to this yet. I haven't had time to think about anything, what with that damned motorcycle gang!" Her fingers now moved through her hair.

"You still worried about them? I mean, really worried about them?"

"Yes, of course I am! You know I am. One of them hurt our son, don't you remember? And Music just threatened us. How many of them do you think might come here to convince me to drop the charges, Sid? And what can we do if they show up?"

Sid sighed. "I don't think we'll have to worry about that. Music's just a good kid gone bad, talking big to save his buddy's neck. But let's not talk about that. Let's discuss us."

"I'm sorry, Sid. I don't think so. Not now." Her expression was tight and resolute.

Sid quietly rose and left the living room. As he walked to the stairs he turned back once to look at Karen. She sat sphinx-like, her hands laid palms down on her thighs, face still, eyes steady.

Michael Fairgate stood in the bathroom, head tilted toward the mirror, surveying the complex bandaging on his head.

"Take it off," Eric urged, tugging at his brother's pajama sleeve. "Let's have a look at it. I bet it's not a 'Z'!"

"How would *you* know?" Michael asked. He gently probed the area, then winced. "Ow! That hurts!"

"Bet it's not a 'Z'!" Eric taunted.

Michael switched off the bathroom light and pushed his bigger brother from the room. "Whatever it is, you're not looking at it tonight. The doctor said we're not supposed to take the bandage off until tomorrow." He spoke solemnly, emphasizing each word.

"Not a 'Z'!"

Michael squinted his eyes, then balled a fist. "I don't care if you *are* older," he said. "Leave me alone. I don't feel good."

The brothers padded into their bedroom.

"Do you think Mom's gonna have another baby?" Eric asked, watching his brother sit on his bed.

"I don't know." Michael's face was shadowed with pain. "Leave me alone. It hurts."

"Sorry," Eric said.

"But I hope she has it."

"Yeah, I guess I do too." Eric pushed his fingers into Michael's ribs."

"Stop it!" Michael yelped, and collapsed into a mass of giggles, the wound and baby forgotten.

Karen walked into her daughter's room. Diana stood in the center of the space, surveying the walls and furniture.

"Mother, I need your objective eye," she said.

"Fine. How was the audition?"

Diana made a face. "They cast the boy's role."

"And?"

"He got second lead."

"Oh."

"So I have to practice some new lines." She continued to look around the room.

"So, what's on your mind?" Karen asked.

"Look at this room," the young woman said.

"Okay." Karen glanced at the girlish room. Everything seemed the same. "So, what about it?"

"Everything looks wrong, somehow." Diana

pursed lips into a slight pout.

"It does? Seems fine to me. You figure it out and let me know." She turned to leave, but Diana grabbed her arm.

"Yes, it was fine, when I was a kid. But I'm not a kid anymore. I'm a woman, and I need a woman's room."

Karen's eyes twinkled. "What, exactly, is a woman's room?"

Diana swept her arms through the air. "Not this," she declared with new-found authority. "Something more worldy, more cosmopolitan, more mature. You know what I mean?"

"What do you want to do, put in a wet bar?"

"No, Mom. It's just that—oh, I don't know." Diana's pout returned.

"You're growing up." Karen gently lifted her daughter's chin with her finger. "Things can be confusing. But don't wish these times away, cookie. You're still sixteen."

"I know but—"

Karen moved her finger to Diana's lips, sealing them, then kissed her cheek and left the room.

Kenny Ward turned his back to Ginger and pulled the sheets up over his body.

"Do you think she'll have it?" Ginger asked.

Kenny yawned. "Who? Have what?"

"Karen. Do you think she'll have the baby?"

"Hell, I don't know." He yawned again and rubbed his prominent chin. "Why should she?"

"I don't know." Ginger puckered her forehead. "I never know what she's thinking these days."

"Then maybe we should get some sleep.

Okay, Ginger? I'm beat.''

She snuggled next to him, but Kenny shifted away from her, finally lying flat on his chest.

Ginger ran her palm down her husband's naked back and felt it rise and fall with his breath. "She's not too old, that's for sure. Women have babies when they're fifty today.''

Kenny sighed and rolled over. "Why's this so important to you? Is that all you can think about?'' He brushed a lock of hair from his eyes.

"No, It's just that—that—'' Ginger broke off the sentence and stared at the ceiling.

"That you want one too?'' Kenny asked, flipping over to his back. He rubbed his eyes. "Is that what you're saying?''

"No!'' Ginger's eyebrows rose. "I never said that.''

"That's all you women ever think about.'' With that Kenny flopped back onto his stomach, eyes shut.

Ginger sighed and touched her stomach. "Can't we talk about this? Just a little?''

"Not again. I'm too tired. Later,'' Kenny said.

Ginger's eyes began to fill. "Okay.''

Chapter Six
Decisions

Gary Ewing walked out of the bathroom into his bedroom, dressed in shorts and a tee-shirt. Val sat on the bed in her silky nightgown, pulling at its hem while she stared down.

"Something wrong, Val?" Gary sat down next to her on the bed.

She shook her head. "It's nothing. I'll be all right."

Gary moved closer. "No, it's not all right. What's bothering you?"

She looked up at Gary, her eyes and cheeks wet. "Oh, Gary, I miss our baby so much!"

"I know," he said, and embraced her.

"If only I could just see her again. It's not fair, what J.R. did to us and to Lucy!"

"That's my brother," Gary said.

"Be serious!" Val picked up her head from his shoulder.

"I'm sorry, honey."

"I know. It's just that Karen, with her new

74

baby, got me to thinking about all this again.''

"You shouldn't, you know." Gary tried to soothe her. "It only makes matters worse and it sure doesn't help you."

"I know." She looked at her husband hopefully, wiping her face and nose with the back of her hand. "Gary, couldn't we start all over again?"

"We are," he said. "That's why we moved to Knots Landing, to get away from all that."

"I know. But do you really want to start over?" She leaned forward slightly, her eyes glistening behind moist eyelashes.

"I don't follow you." He cocked his head almost to his shoulder.

"Oh, Gary, why don't we have another baby?"

"What?"

"Sure. It would be just what I need to really start my life over. Just what *we* need. It'll take my mind off so many things. Oh, Gary, can't we?"

He looked at her in shock, then grinned. "We sure can think about it," he said, and added swiftly, "You're not pregnant, are you?"

She shook her head and lowered her eyes. "No. I wouldn't do that to you, without telling you." Her voice was hushed.

He sighed. "I'm sorry, but what with Karen surprising Sid and the rest of us, you can't be too sure."

"I know." She looked wistful. "Well, at least we talked about it." Val sighed. "That's something. And you will think about it?"

"Sure," Gary said gravely. "I don't know if I'm ready for that responsibility . . ."

"I understand." Val almost whispered. "Still, it would be wonderful."

Music puffed on a cigarette as he sat in the visiting room at the Knots Landing Police Station. He pushed the crumpled red box along the edge of the Formica-topped table. Damn, he thought. They said he could see Alien. So where the hell was he? Music blew blue smoke through the wire grating behind which his friend was supposed to materialize.

He crushed out his cigarette and stood. A door opened and handcuffs clanked as Alien walked into the room behind the wire grate, pushed along by a mammoth, beefy, uniformed officer with a crewcut and a shining billy club.

"All right, man, just leave me and my friend," Alien grumbled. He rustled the handcuffs that secured his wrists behind his back. "Got me locked up, Music."

"Sit down, punk," the officer said.

Music sat on his side of the grating as Alien slid into the chair.

"Alien, good buddy." Music smiled. "How are you feelin', man?"

"How do you think I'm feeling?" he snarled. "You gotta get me out of here, Music! You gotta!" Alien's eyes were red, wild.

Music glanced at the officer, who stood four feet behind Alien's right shoulder, arms crossed and propped up on a massive chest.

"Hang easy, Alien," he said and grimaced at the officer. "You'll make it."

"Hell, I don't care about *him*," the bearded biker said, lowering his voice. "What about the broad? Will she drop the charges against me and let me outa here?''

"That's just it, old buddy. She won't.''

"Why?''

"She's sliding all over you. Won't give an inch. I tried to talk her into it last night, but she threatened to lock me up.'' He pressed his hand on the grating. "It don't look so good, man.''

Alien slammed his fist against his forehead. "Damn!''

"Hey, Alien, it's not all bad.''

"Yeah?'' he snapped, eyes piercing. "You should try staying in here.''

"You've only been in there a while, but I feel for you, buddy. I really do.''

"Yeah? How about getting me the hell out of this place?''

"There might be a way. Maybe we can *persuade* her to drop the charge against you.''

Alien scratched his chin. "How?''

"Leave that to me,'' Music muttered, glancing at the guard. "I can be very persuasive, can't I?''

"Sure.'' Alien's eyes lit up. "Yeah?''

"Yeah. Me and the boys will talk some sense into her, you know what I mean?''

Alien appeared calmer.

"Besides, you know my way with women. She'll melt like butter in my hands.'' Music smirked.

"Like butter,'' Alien said, and grunted. He leaned closer to the grating. "Watch yourself, ol' buddy. That broad's a tough nut to crack.''

"Relax, Alien. Don't be so tense. I'll get you out of here. Don't worry about that.''

"I can't stand it anymore, Music!'' Alien began

to whine again. "I can't stand it!" His face was twisted with rage. "I'm going crazy. I don't care what it takes—just do it so they let me out of this damn place."

"Hey, watch that mouth of yours, punk!" the officer said, his voice high and twangy.

Alien wrestled with the cuffs. "Get me out of these things!" he yelled.

"Okay, visiting hours are over." The officer gripped Alien's trapped arms with his fleshy paws and hurled him, screaming, toward the door.

Music watched as his friend was pushed through the doorway and out of the room, then shook his head. He pulled a cigarette from the pack and lit it with a glittery, abalone shell-covered lighter. Alien is in a bad way, he thought.

The biker shuffled out of the police station, keeping his head low as a multitude of uniformed officers walked past him. He held his breath until he was out the front doors, standing in the cool California sea air, watching the moon's reflection in a puddle of water on the street.

He would convince the woman to drop the charges, Music swore as he headed for his bike. As he walked up to it he noticed the deep scratches along the gas tank, the broken headlamp, the twisted metal.

That woman had hurt his bike and got his friend locked up. Music slammed his fist into his palm as he straddled the black seat cushion. She's asking for it, Music thought. That damn woman is asking for it. But I'll go slow at first. No sense in wasting the heavy ammunition at first. If she doesn't change her mind, I'll rough her up *good*.

An idea crossed his mind. Music beamed as he sat on the motorcycle. Her daughter. She had a young, beautiful daughter. That *was* an idea to think about. Music blasted the engines and raced away from the police station.

Karen Fairgate tapped her temple with the eraser-end of a pencil. Nestled around her elbows on her desk were stacks of papers. She peered intently into the open ledger before her, then jotted a few figures down.

It was late, but Karen needed to know some things before she could sleep. Giving birth to a child was something to be considered from all aspects. Her latest angle—volunteer work.

Karen shook her head and yawned.

"Coming upstairs?" Sid asked from behind her. He leaned over and kissed the back of her neck.

"In a minute. I have to finish this first."

"Okay."

She felt Sid behind her, his breath streaming across her right ear as he bent to look.

"What are you doing?" He bent closer.

"In a minute." She pushed him away and, turning toward her calculator, punched in several figures. Seconds later Karen nodded, then entered the figures in the ledger.

"Not bad, huh?" she asked, looking at Sid.

"Pretty good."

She sighed. "There's no way around it."

"Around what?" Sid nuzzled her.

"If I become a mother again, the A.C.L.U.'s going to have to make do with several thousand dollars less next year than last year."

"Why?" Sid asked. He straightened up, then sat on the edge of the desk.

"I can't raise the funds. Not if I'm going to have a baby. This is one of the things I have to consider."

Sid looked puzzled. "I don't see why you can't. You've done fund-raising from here before."

She pushed the ledger aside. "That's not the problem. It's a matter of energy. I wouldn't have *any* right now if I'd been changing diapers and burping babies all day."

"Okay, you're probably right about that," Sid said.

"There's no way."

"At least it's not as if you have a career—" Sid began, then broke off the sentence.

Karen looked up at him violently. "I don't?" she asked, her voice crisp.

"Honey, you know what I mean."

"No, I don't. Tell me."

"Come on, Karen. It's—"

"Just because I do volunteer work doesn't mean I don't have a career!" Karen stood, her back stiff. "I take all this very seriously, Sid. Someone has to help them."

"I know you take them seriously, but—"

She interrupted, "But since I don't bring home a paycheck I don't have a career. Right?"

Sid frowned. "I didn't say that." He slipped off the desk to his feet.

"You didn't have to. I have three children

growing up in a dirty, corrupt world. I'm trying to make that world better for them.''

"There's nothing wrong with that, sweetheart," Sid said.

"To me, that's more important than becoming a corporate vice-president or something. And it's certainly more important to the future of the world.''

"Of course," Sid agreed quietly.

She looked at him. "Maybe—maybe it's the most important thing I can do right now. I like to think I'm making a difference.''

"No one said you weren't," Sid said, his voice soft.

Karen exhaled audibly. "I don't know, Sid. I just don't know. Maybe it's more important than becoming a mother again." She turned toward the stairs.

"Karen," Sid walked toward her. "Can't we finish this?''

"Do me a favor, Sid." Karen spoke in hard, unyielding tones. "Stay down here for a while. I can't take any more of your helpful looks or grudging support.''

"But Karen—''

"Give me some room, Sid," Karen snapped and quickly walked up the stairs.

Chapter Seven
Chaos In the Cul-de-sac

A mourning dove cooed in the peaceful sunrise. As the light increased, the Seaview Circle cul-de-sac glistened with dew, and crystalline droplets fell from the trashcans that lined the curb.

The dove's coos faded in the grindingly mechanical noise of an approaching garbage truck. It halted at the curb and two men in plastic clothing grabbed the waiting cans.

Halfway through emptying the first can, the shorter of the two looked up at his partner. "I'm tired of garbage. I'm tired of how it looks, how it smells, how it feels." He frowned. "You know what I mean? I never want to see another can again."

The other man, red-haired and wiry, laughed. "Sure. I think the same thing every morning when I have to get up while it's still dark outside. But I still show for work, and you will too."

"A lot you know, Harrington. Some day you'll show up for work and I won't be there. I'm ready to quit right now.''

Harrington snorted. ''Sure, Glover. You've been saying that for years now. Get back to work.''

Glover shrugged and emptied the can, then swung it back down to the curb. He stood watching as the garbage was crushed and then disappeared from the loading bin.

Damn garbage, he thought, and poured out the second can.

''Come on! We're fifteen minutes behind schedule, Glover!''

He turned to replace the can on the sidewalk, then dropped it and leapt back. A red motorcycle, its driver outfitted in leather and Levis, shot down the sidewalk past him.

''Whoa!'' he gasped. As Glover watched, the cyclist veered from the sidewalk onto the downy-soft, irridescent lawns, ripping up patches of dark earth.

Two more cycles shot into the cul-de-sac as Glover pressed back against the truck, watching.

''Can those boys ride or what, Harrington?'' Glover's eyes were wide with awe.

''Let's get the hell out of here.'' Harrington backed to the door.

''Come on—let me watch the show.''

The gang formed a tight circle of roaring cycles, then branched out and seemed to strike at will. One black-haired female biker, her thighs clinging to those of an unshaven, short-haired rider, produced a rock from her purse and threw it at the nearest window. It shattered. The girl whinnied a strange, high-pitched laugh and lobbed another.

"Man, am I getting out of here!" Harrington said.

"All right, all right." Glover climbed up into the cab. "Wow! Great view from up here!" He wiped sweat from his forehead and watched. "Look—there goes that one. Pow!"

The front wheel of the red bike nicked a full trash can, sending it spinning and pelting garbage over the yard and sidewalk in front of the Averys' home.

Harrington gunned the garbage truck's engines. "You're weird, you know that, Glover?"

"It's them."

Sid was halfway down stairs before Karen was on her feet running from the bed. The roar of the motorcycles continue to echo through the cul-de-sac, peppered with crashes and metallic bangs. The cacophony increased to booming proportions.

"It sounds like World War III out there," Karen said, wrapping her robe around her body as she passed the bottom of the stairs. She rushed up to the front door as Sid unlocked it.

"Stay here!" he demanded, putting up his arm to block her.

"Like hell I will!" Karen pushed past him and ran outside. On the porch, Karen stopped, then stepped back, her hand to her mouth.

The motorcycles dipped and wove around them, spinning a web of destruction through the neighborhood. Booted feet knocked over the few still standing garbage cans.

"Where's Music?" Karen wondered aloud,

standing beside Sid, shivering in the cool morning air.

Sid scanned the bikes. "I don't see him. Must not have shown. You've seen enough. Get back inside, Karen!"

"He's got to be here."

Sid pushed her inside and slammed the door shut, then ran out to the sidewalk. A biker quickly zoomed past him, sending his hair and robe flapping.

"Stop it!" he yelled. "Leave us alone!"

The center of the street exploded as hundreds of firecrackers shot off into life. The pops seemed to whip up the bikers' enthusiasm and they sped faster around the cul-de-sac. A rock fragmented a car's rear window.

"Damn you!" Sid shouted. He noticed the other Seaview Circle homeowners, who stood on their porches, watching.

With the precision of a flock of birds the motorcycles merged into an orderly unit of three and, revving their engines, sped from the cul-de-sac.

Sid waited until the sound of the motorcycles had died, then stomped back into his house.

Twenty minutes later Sergeant Willis sat sipping steaming coffee in the Fairgate living room, with many of the cul-de-sac's residents seated around him.

"What are you saying, Wayne?" Sid's voice cracked with strain. "Are you telling us that there's nothing you can do? Our neighborhood has been terrorized and you can't stop it from happening again?"

"No, Sid," Willis said, shaking his head. "I'm

just saying that they've got an advantage on us."

"How?" Karen asked.

"Motorcycles can go places our cars can't. That makes it a lot tougher on us. There's lots of hiding places around here."

"Terrific," Karen said with disgust, seated beside her husband on the couch. "So we just put up with it?"

Willis set down his coffee. "We'll make sure our cars patrol here regularly. I'll do everything I can to see that you folks are safe here."

Karen glanced at Val and Gary Ewing, who sat on the love seat. Valene tried to smile, but she looked tired and distraught.

"Well, no matter what happens, I'm not dropping that charge," Karen asserted. "I can't." Her voice was hard with conviction.

Richard Avery clenched his jaw. "Listen, Laura and I moved here to get away from things like this. We pay higher taxes in Knots Landing for better protection." His upper lip was pale.

"That's right," Willis countered. "A lot of people have moved here for that reason. So many that we can't take care of them all. The population of Knots Landing has almost doubled in the last ten years. And you know how much the police department has grown? We've gone from ten to twelve patrol cars."

Richard smirked. "That's not very reassuring."

"We'll get them," Willis said, and dismissed Richard with a wave.

"Thanks, Wayne," Sid said. "We know you're doing everything in your power."

"Take care, folks." Willis left.

Richard moved closer to Sid as the sergeant

exited. "I'm worried," he said.

"Why?"

"I don't know, Sid. This could be just the beginning. You think about that?" He looked at Karen. "These guys are having fun. They'll probably be back."

Gary Ewing cleared his throat. "What are you suggesting, Richard? That Karen drop the charge? You're a lawyer—you should be able to give us some good advice."

Richard nodded. "Yeah, I'm a lawyer, and I know the limitations of the law." He gestured toward the door. "If more of them start coming in like they've threatened to, and if Willis can't do anything about it—I'd say we're in a real bind." He glanced quickly at his watch. "I'd better get back to Laura and Jason."

"How are they?" Val asked.

"Scared, but fine. Bye."

He left with a short wave.

Karen lay back on the couch. "He thinks I should give in."

Gary laughed. "Come on, Karen. Of course he does. Richard thinks only about what's best for Richard. He's worried about the garbage on his car."

Karen looked up to see Eric, Michael and Diana standing quietly behind the adults. "Come on, kids. Upstairs. Get ready for school. It's business as usual, despite the circus this morning."

Reluctantly the three headed up the stairs. Karen's eyes followed them as they left.

"I'm not thinking of this as a cause," Karen said, turning toward her husband. "This isn't some wild fling, fulfilling some need of mine to be involved and feel productive.''

"I'd be the first to tell you if it was, honey," Sid said with affection.

"I know it's tough on everybody, especially the kids," Karen began.

"Don't be crazy." Sid tapped her on the shoulder. "It'd be a lot worse if they saw you letting those thugs have their way."

"I'm glad you won't give in, Karen," Val encouraged.

Karen turned to look at her. "You okay, Val? You haven't been talking much this morning."

Val nodded, sending her blonde hair swinging. "I'm fine. And you are doing the right thing, not giving in to them. Maybe the police here in Knots Landing aren't perfect, and they aren't going to catch those guys in fifteen minutes, but at least they're on our side. That's something."

"But Val, of course they're on our side," Karen said, perplexed.

"They're not always." She drew her lips together.

Sid slid forward on the couch. "What was that?"

Val looked at Gary guardedly. "Just that they're not always on the side I'm on." She lowered her head. "Nothing. I shouldn't be talking about this."

Gary took her hand and intertwined their fingers. "It's okay, honey," he said softly. "You can tell them."

Val pushed back her hair and sighed. "When Gary and I were married the first time and then split up—seventeen years ago . . . I left Lucy to be brought up by her grandparents and his brother J.R. One day I stopped by to visit and take Lucy out for a ride—and J.R. turned on me! He sent some mean old boys to my place and had Lucy brought back to the ranch—as if I weren't her mother! So I went to the sheriff's office."

Gary Ewing shifted uncomfortably on the loveseat next to his wife. "Uh . . . My family's pretty tight with the law."

"I can't tell you what that was like," Val said, "knowing that J.R. could do anything to me and there wasn't anything the police could, or would, do about it. There wasn't any difference between those old boys and the police." She tried to blink away the memories. "That's why I said what I did. But at least here there *is* a difference. Old J.R. doesn't have his hands on the local law. They're on our side. Even if it's hard for you, Karen, I think you should stick to your guns."

"Thanks. I do too, Val," Karen said.

"Am I makin' any sense at all?" Val asked nervously.

Karen rose and walked to her. "Plenty," she assured her, squeezing her arm.

"Well, we should be going," Gary said, rising. He took Val's hand and they walked toward the door. "Keep us posted on what you hear from Sergeant Willis."

"I will," Sid promised.

"Thanks again, Val." Karen blew her a kiss as they left.

Richard winced through another swallow of hot coffee. "This is lousy," he complained, setting the cup on the table.

"Sorry." Laura's eyes were downcast. "I won't buy that brand again."

"I sure hope my insurance covers things like this," he said, looking through the window at the mess outside.

Laura set her cup on the saucer before her. "The car just needs a good washing, honey," she said gently. "I'll hose it off while you and Jason have breakfast."

"How is Jason anyway? Is he okay?"

"Yes. Full of questions, but he's quiet now. He's getting ready for school." She paused. "What happened at the Fairgates while the police were there?"

"Nothing," Richard said with irritation, then sipped the coffee again. "She won't budge. Willis and the police can't do a damn thing, and Karen refuses to drop the charge against Alien. She's going to get us all killed."

"Richard!" Laura said. "That's a little over-dramatic."

"Is it?" He stared into his coffee sullenly.

"Besides, she's taking this more personally than we are. Her son was hurt."

"He's hurt himself worse on his skateboard, Laura."

Laura looked at him critically. "And suppose it was Jason who'd been hurt."

"It wasn't," he said, and drained the cup.

"Look, I think you're overreacting."

Richard slammed the cup on the counter.

When the kids had left for school and their living room had emptied, Karen and Sid stood at the door.

"You okay, honey?" Sid asked, straightening his striped tie.

"Sure. I was just thinking about the baby."

Sid froze momentarily, then slid his hands down from his tie. "What were you thinking?" he asked, trying to sound casual.

"If I don't have this baby, I'll always wonder what it might have looked like, who it would have grown up to be, all those things I missed." The corners of her mouth turned down. "But if I do have it, I'll ask the same questions—about *me*."

"You?" Sid asked.

"Sure. I'd wonder what I could have done, who I could have become, and everything I missed out on."

"Karen," Sid sympathized. "I know what you're going through."

"This battle this morning was the last thing I needed right now. It hasn't helped me a bit in figuring out what I should do. And I can't go through many more days without making a decision."

"It's been so tough on you," he said tenderly.

"That's an understatement."

"So what are you trying to say, Karen?"

She exhaled deeply. "Don't you see, Sid? I can't have this baby, and I can't *not* have it."

Chapter Eight
Pressure

Richard Avery was on his knees on the lawn, trying to repair the damage done by the bikes. He wiped his forehead and glanced at his wife.

"Can you believe that about the Fairgates?" he asked, rising to his feet.

"Believe what?" Laura squirted a hose on newly planted flowers in their front yard.

"The baby—Karen pregnant."

"Oh. I don't know—things like that happen." Laura smiled swiftly and kept her eyes lowered.

"Old Sid," Richard huffed, dusting off his hands. "Who would have thought it?"

Laura watched as the water darkened the earth around the neatly planted flowers. "He's not that old, Richard. And neither is Karen."

Richard frowned as he saw another area that had been messed up by the gang. "It's not just that," he said, carefully raking the area. "What really threw me was that they seemed so settled in their lives. They sure caught me by surprise."

Laura nodded slightly, glanced at her husband, then returned her attention to the hose.

"I guess it's never too late," he mused, his back to his wife. "We could even do it."

"Do what?" She sounded distracted.

"You know, Laura. Have another baby."

Laura almost dropped the hose and stared at the back of her husband's head. "We *could*?"

Richard turned to her. "Of course we could. There's nothing wrong with us physically. We're young, healthy—what more do we need?"

"Money," Laura said simply.

"Money? Hey, we're living comfortably."

"We're only now getting on our feet," Laura reminded him.

Richard scowled. "Right. This might be the perfect time to have an addition to the Avery family. Jason needs someone to play with. I don't want him to be an only child."

Laura lifted the hose again and sprayed the grass. "It's something to think about," she remarked and concentrated on the lawn.

"It sure is. Not a bad idea, I think. Another little Avery underfoot. I kind of miss that." Richard's voice was unusually sincere. He looked at his wife intently.

She continued to keep her eyes lowered but nodded slightly as she watched the grass.

"What do you think, Laura?" Richard pressed.

"Like I said, something to think about."

He rested his hands on his hips and stared at his wife. "That's all? Just something to think about?"

"Honey," she began.

"I'm being serious here, you know. I'm not just talking. I think we should have another baby—another son."

Laura's tone became strained. "Not now, okay? With all the trouble in the neighborhood I can't talk about it now. Please?"

He sighed. "Oh, okay, Laura." Richard spotted some deep ruts at the far end of the lawn. "Damn," he muttered, walking over. He looked down at the damage, trying to figure the best way to repair it. Then, turning back to his wife, he said, "Just remember—*I'm* thinking about it."

Karen maneuvered her overloaded shopping cart past the frozen foods aisle on the way to the checkout counter while Val walked beside her.

"Val, I guess that's about it for me."

"I'm done too." Val surveyed her less than half-full cart, comparing it to Karen's. She frowned. "You have to do a lot more shopping when you have a big family," she said longingly.

"Don't I know it," Karen answered, then pressed her lips together. "I'm sorry, Val. I didn't mean to—"

"It's okay," she said. "Lucy's gone right now, but I'll get her back some day. I'm not gonna let that old J.R. keep her forever."

"Have you thought about having another child?" Karen asked, opening her purse to check her cash as they waited their turn at the checkout counter.

"Sure," Val replied. "I've thought about it a lot. But Gary's not ready right now. I don't blame him, I guess, but I miss—" Val's face became lined with pain.

"Maybe we should finish this conversation somewhere else," Karen suggested quickly.

Val nodded.

They went through the line in silence. Afterward they left the supermarket and walked outside, pushing their carts toward Karen's station wagon.

"I feel a little better now, a little safer. Seeing those patrol cars drive by the cul-de-sac every twenty minutes gives me some sense of security," Karen said.

"I guess the worst is over."

"You mean you *hope* the worst is over," Karen gently corrected her. They stopped before Karen's car. "Who would have dreamed that something like what happened this morning could take place in Knots Landing?"

"Hello, ladies," a familiar voice said behind them.

Karen and Val turned sharply. "You!" Karen's voice oozed contempt.

"Me." Music stood before her, grinning mischievously.

"Karen, careful . . ." Val cautioned.

"What the hell do you want? Haven't you done enough? The neighborhood's in shambles."

"Hey," Music assumed an expression of innocence. "I didn't have anything to do with what happened this morning, now did I?"

"I'll bet!" Karen snarled, her face crimson.

"Hey—I tried to stop them but they wouldn't listen to me. They'll only listen to Alien."

"Karen, let's get out of here," Val pleaded.

"Music, why don't you and your boys leave

town? You're not welcome here. We're tired of your games, we don't want to play them anymore, and, in case you didn't notice, we don't like you."

"I'm hurt." Music pursed his lips with mock sorrow, and flipped out a pack of cigarettes. He lit one quickly.

"Let's go," Val urged Karen.

"Just leave us alone!" Karen left her shopping cart at the rear of the car and, with a look to Music, opened the doors.

Music reached into Karen's cart.

"What are you doing?" she shouted, turning around.

He pulled an apple from one of the sacks and bit into it. Juice ran down his chin.

"Tasty . . ." he licked his lips, staring directly at Karen, then turned and casually walked toward his motorcycle, which was parked in the far corner of the parking lot.

"Let's load these up," Karen started hauling bags into the back seats.

"How can you be so calm?" Val marveled.

"He wasn't with the ones this morning," Karen noted.

"But you didn't believe him when he said—"

"No, of course not. But what could I have done? He would have been long gone before I could even call the police." She pushed her last bag into the car and then stuffed Val's in beside them. Karen slammed the door shut. "Come on, let's get out of here."

A minute later Karen drove toward Seaview Circle. "Music doesn't scare me," Karen explained. "His friends might, but not him."

Val shivered. "I don't like him. He just seems so—well, *evil*."

"I'm not fond of him myself," Karen said, "but I won't let him scare me." She smiled defiantly and glanced into the rear-view mirror before changing lanes. Her smile faded. "Oh, no," she groaned.

"What is it?"

"Look behind you, Val."

Val turned. She gasped.

Through the rear view window she saw two women on motorcycles rapidly gaining on Karen's car.

"Karen, it's them! I recognize the black-haired one."

"I know," she said.

"What can we do?"

The sound of the engines filled the air as the bikes pulled up alongside Karen's car. The woman with black hair gunned her motorcycle, then tilted it perilously close to Karen's right fender.

"Karen!" Val cried out in warning as she clutched her seat.

"Hang on!" Karen checked the rear-view mirror, saw that the lane behind her was empty, and slammed down on the brakes. The female cyclist shot forward past them as her tires screeched.

"Whoa!" Val blanched as her breath caught in her throat.

"We'll make it." Karen thrust her foot down on the gas pedal. "We're almost home."

The bikers slowed up ahead, then crossed the street's center line and raced back toward Karen.

As they approached, the bikes switched lanes and soon roared up directly toward Karen's station wagon.

Karen held her ground. Val's fingernails dug into the seat but she kept quiet. Just before they would have collided with the car the two motorcycles veered and continued on down the road away from her.

Val Ewing squeezed her eyes shut and held her grip on the seat cushion. "Tell me when we're there," she said.

Karen sighed. "I think they left." She scanned the mirrors, then looked over her shoulder.

The road was clear behind them, save for a shining silver Mercedes-Benz.

"Those women are as bad as the men," Val concluded.

"They sure are." Karen checked the rear-view mirror again. "They're also coming back."

"No!" Val cried, her eyes still tightly shut. "What are you going to do?"

"I don't know," she said. "But we'll do something. Just hang on!"

The air was cut with the rips of engines and the roar of the wind as Karen pushed more firmly on the gas. The cyclists appeared closer behind her. Karen increased her speed to an unsafe sixty miles per hour.

The pair of cyclists wove from side to side in the lane behind her as Karen saw the next turn she had to make. As the bikers gained on her, Karen swallowed as she slowed and turned the wheel sharply to the left, automatically braking to ease the car through the turn. She sighed as the brakes squealed, then silenced themselves.

The bikers had managed to follow her through the turn. They were again on each side of the car. Val turned and looked at the face of the female biker beside her. The woman's mouth curled and she banged her bike against the car door. Val screamed.

"It's okay, it's okay," Karen insisted, her eyes fixed on the entrance to Seaview Circle ahead.

"How are you going to turn?" Val's voice was shrill with terror. "They won't let you." She looked at the bike jockeying beside her, its gas tank so close that Val could have reached out and touched the gleaming metal.

"I don't know," Karen admitted.

A harsh bump on the left front fender jolted Val. The woman on the bike shouted something, but Karen couldn't hear it through the noise of the engines. Three hundred yards from the entrance to Seaview Circle a patrol car pulled into sight.

"Karen!" Val exclaimed.

"I know!" She pounded on the horn repeatedly.

The patrol car flashed its lights and sped toward them. The two cycles instantly turned and raced off in the opposite direction, the police car pursuing them.

"Boy, am I glad that's over." The skin on Val's face was visibly damp. "It's too much like the movies for me, boy."

Karen drove much too quickly toward her driveway, and had to apply her brakes forcefully to halt her station wagon as it bounced up and approached the garage door.

Val wiped her forehead as the car stopped. She

clutched her chest. "Am I glad that police car was there," she said. "And that it was on our side."

Karen smiled briefly—her hands felt glued to the steering wheel. "You and me both. Come on, let's get these groceries put away." She opened her hands and stretched her aching fingers. They quickly unloaded the car and went into the house.

"Karen, I can go on home by myself, really," Val argued as they stood, holding her two bags.

"No, you can't. I'll call Sid and have him bring Gary back here with him."

The phone rang. Karen picked it up.

"Mrs. Fairgate?" a low voice said.

"Yes. Who is this?' Karen's eyes narrowed.

"You know who. You better let Alien out of jail, bitch."

Karen stiffened. "And if I don't?"

"Who is it?" Val whispered.

He laughed. "This morning wasn't even a taste of what'll happen to you."

"You're not scaring me," she said firmly.

"Not yet. We will. But there's an easy way to get us to leave you alone. Drop the charge."

"No way," she persisted.

The man seemed to hiss. "Okay. You asked for it."

Karen slammed down the phone.

"Was it them?" Val asked, knowing it was.

Karen nodded. "Same old story," she said. "Trying to talk me into letting Alien go free." Her breath puffed from her parted lips.

"I kind of figured that."

"I'm calling Sid," Karen said, and lifted the receiver again. As she put it to her ear she heard an earthy laugh.

"Couldn't stop talking to me, couldja?" the biker taunted.

"Stop it!" Karen screamed. "Hang up or I'll—I'll—" She threw the receiver into its cradle again.

Val set a bag of groceries on the table. "What are we going to do?"

Karen blinked repeatedly, her face awash with misery. "I don't know, Val. I just don't know."

"For starters, you could get that ice cream into the freezer," Val said softly.

Karen turned to look at it. A thin stream of vanilla trailed out from one of the shopping bags on the counter. She frowned, and cupped her face with her limp hands.

The two female bikers drove off the road into a secluded, wooded point high above the pounding Pacific Ocean. There, amid the trees and dense brush, Music sat alone smoking as the two women pulled up.

"We did it!' Mary bragged.

"Anyone hurt?"

"No. But we sure scared the hell out of them. Didn't we, Alison?"

"Yeah. Easy as pie."

"Well," Music said, and inhaled. "Glad to know you're good for something, Mary."

She smiled sarcastically and ran a hand through her dyed black hair. "You're a pistol, you know that, Music? You really are. You think you're God's gift to women." She smirked. "What a joke!"

"Come on, Mary," Allison said. "Let's go

swimming." She started to unbutton her blouse.

"You go. Get lost, Alison. Now—" Mary ordered, then turned to Music.

"All right, all right. Jeez!" Alison continued unbuttoning as she ambled off toward the beach.

Mary stared at Music.

"Why'd you get rid of Alison?" Music asked.

"We don't need her."

"Did you make a clean break of it today?"

Mary frowned. "Not quite. A police car chased us from her street to half-way across town. But we lost him without too much sweat. We're good riders." She looked around their primitive camp. "So where's Ross?"

"Out," Music said, puffing on a cigarette. "I sent him into town to get some food and beer. I figured we should eat today."

"Damn!" Mary kicked the ground.

"What's wrong? Miss your lover? Jealous he's taken up with Alison?"

She turned back to him and sneered. "Me? I think you're jealous of Ross. Cause he's had both of us."

"You're dreaming, man," Music said.

"So how about it?" Mary moved over to him. She sat on the rock, her thigh against his.

"How about what?" he asked, bored.

"You and me? I thought we might—"

Music shrugged. "Whatever. It's no big deal to me."

"Thanks a lot!" Mary said.

"Nothing personal, but I don't feel like it right now." Music stood up, restless.

"Okay, okay," Mary said, testy but not wanting to fight. "Wish you'd change your mind."

"Look, woman!" Music barked. "I just can't handle it right now. I've got too much on my mind—Alien in the slammer, that Fairgate broad not giving in . . ."

Mary raised an eyebrow. "Who said anything about you handling me?"

Music slammed his fist against his thigh. "I don't need your games. That might keep Ross happy, but not me. Got it?" He frowned. "I don't care if you sleep with the whole club. Just leave me alone."

"Alien said you had trouble with women, sometimes," she said softly.

Music turned and grabbed her arm. "Alien said what?" He yanked the arm down, sending Mary yelping. "You're lying to me, slut!" Music's usually handsome face was puffy, slick with sweat, and veined. "Tell me you're lying! Alien wouldn't say—"

"Okay, okay, it must have been someone else who said it," Mary struggled to free herself.

"You—" Music looked at her in astonishment, then broke into laughter. He pulled her roughly toward him. Mary's body pressed up against his. "You little tease. You'd say anything to get a guy you want, wouldn't you?"

"Yeah." Her lips slightly parted, she nibbled against his unshaven cheek, across his chin and down his neck.

"I like guys," Mary coaxed. "And I like you."

"Tell me about it," Music said, pulling her more tightly against him. "Tell me all about it."

Chapter Nine

Harassment

Laura Avery shifted her car into reverse and started backing down her driveway. The car wobbled as she began rolling, and a curious popping noise seemed to emanate from the tires. Confused, Laura halted her car and got out to investigate. She bent down to examine the front left tire. It was flat.

"Oh, no," she said aloud, and headed for the trunk and the jack. On her way there she noticed that the left rear tire was also flat. Curious, she walked around the car—all four tires were devoid of air.

"Those bikers!" she bristled, pounding the hood with her fist. "Wait until Karen hears about this." Laura hurriedly headed for the Fairgate home, then stopped when she saw a man squatting before Karen's station wagon. The man pulled a knife from the tire and rose, then started toward the Ewings' home.

Laura watched him in disbelief—the man was

vandalizing their cars in broad daylight. "Hey, what do you think you're doing?" she shouted.

The biker turned, looked her up and down and flashed the knife in her direction. "What the hell do you want?" He took a few steps toward her.

Laura stumbled back. "Nothing!" she said, and ran toward Karen's house. She pounded on the door.

"What is it?" Karen asked after opening it.

Laura pointed at the biker, who calmly and systematically slashed Val's car tires.

Karen looked at Laura. "Go back to your house, will you, and call the police, then Richard, Sid and Gary. My phone's not working. Get them all home. Now!"

"Okay," she said, and hurried out as Val came in.

The biker ran from the cul-de-sac on foot.

"Punk!" Karen yelled. She walked back into the house to check the phone. She picked it up but the line was still dead. "We might not have a phone, but Laura does. She's calling the men."

"What happened?" Val asked.

"Some biker just gave us all flats. Laura, you and me." She glowered. "I don't believe this. That pig was out there with his knife cutting the tires and smiling. He was smiling while he was doing it!"

"They just won't quit," Val despaired.

The distant roar of a motorcycle filtered in through the open windows.

Val looked at Karen. "Stick to your guns." Her voice was firm and consoling. "You've got to do what you feel is right."

"I guess." Karen looked utterly dispirited.

Laura walked into Karen's living room without knocking. "They're on their way," she announced.

"How long are they going to do this to us?" Karen murmured.

"I don't know," Laura said. "Richard thinks they won't let up until Alien's free."

Karen grimaced. "Richard—he's some character, your husband," she said sarcastically.

Laura blushed. "I know. He's an—interesting person."

"He seems kinda nice," Val considered, "but he doesn't want to show it." She straightened her shoulders and patted Karen's back. "I still think you shouldn't give in to them, Karen. That's why J.R.'s causing so much trouble back home in Texas—folks are afraid of him, so they let him walk all over them."

Laura looked toward the window, her mouth tense. "I just hope that Sid's right, that they move on without Alien."

"I don't think they will, Laura. Music said something about Alien being their leader. If that's true, they won't budge without him." Karen sighed. "Why now? As if I don't have other things to worry about." She patted her stomach.

"About that—" Laura said. "Richard's started bugging me about having a baby, thanks to you," she complained goodnaturedly.

"Look what you started." Val smiled.

"He's only mentioned it once, but I've never seen him so—so *honest* about something with me."

"That's a good start," Karen said.

"Have you made up your mind yet about, well, you know?" Val asked Karen.

"No. Not yet. I haven't had much time to think about it, what with all the excitement lately."

"Whatever you do, you can count on us," Val assured her. "Isn't that right, Laura?"

"Of course!"

Karen gazed at them gratefully. "Thanks. The baby seems so far off, though. Maybe it would be better to get Alien and his gang out of town before I make any commitments."

"That could take weeks," Laura despaired.

"Don't even think that! No, I'll drop the charges if things like this keep up, or if they get worse. I can't put the whole cul-de-sac and the beach through hell just because I'm stubborn."

"You're standing up for your rights," Val reminded her.

"And the whole cul-de-sac's the worse for it." Karen folded her arms.

"At least they haven't tried to hurt us," Val said, "except for Michael."

A small crash followed by the screams of two children pierced their conversation.

"That was outside." Karen ran toward the door. "If they've hurt Eric or Michael!"

Laura and Val ran after her.

Outside, Karen's sons lay sprawled on the street, face down, their bicycles askew nearby. The blacktop was covered with a dark, shining substance.

"Are you all right?" Karen yelled frantically as she approached them.

"Yeah," Eric began to rub his knee. His pants darkened where he rubbed.

"What happened?" Karen asked.

"We slipped while we were riding our bikes. There's oil all over the street." He got up with effort.

"Is that what that is?" Karen touched the substance. "Oil?"

"A whole canful, it looks like," Michael said. "Be careful, Mom." He now stood beside his brother.

"But you're okay? Both of you?" Karen studied her children for a moment.

"I guess so," Eric said.

"Good. Get inside."

"What?" Eric asked.

"Leave the bikes. Clean the oil off your shoes and get inside the house!"

"But Mom," Michael began.

"You heard me, didn't you? Leave your bikes and get inside! Now!"

Eric looked at his brother, rolled his eyes, and followed him to the grass, where they wiped the oil off their shoes, then went into the house.

Karen hugged her shoulders, her face a battleground of fiery emotions.

Val touched Karen's back gently. "Karen?"

She continued to stare out into the street.

"Are you okay?" Val asked.

"No," she said, then broke down, her sobs soundless, her entire body trembling.

After Val Ewing and Laura Avery left the house later that afternoon, Richard Avery pushed Sid out to the garage on the pretext of checking the timing on Sid's classic Chevy. "I'm sure it was a little off," Richard said, and smiled sweetly to Karen.

Karen waved them off as they left the living room.

Once inside the garage Sid flicked on the lights. The red Chevrolet gleamed. "What was this about the timing? You know I just checked it."

"Just an excuse," Richard said.

"I figured." Sid Fairgate lifted the hood and propped it up. "At least we can look like we're working." He bent over the engine. "What's up, Richard?"

Richard moved to the other side of the car. "It's Karen. How much longer can she hold out? I mean, the neighborhood's been terrorized, windows have been broken, the beach is practically a battleground . . ." His voice trailed off.

Sid was silent for a moment. "I don't know. I'm not sure what she's thinking these days."

"What will it take to get through to her? These guys are just playing around now, Sid. You know that. But I don't think Karen knows what they're capable of doing. We're not talking high school delinquents here. She's endangering herself, her family, the whole neighborhood."

"Don't you think I know that?" Sid's gaze pierced Richard's eyes. "She knows it too. Karen's confused, and she's got every right to be."

"You mean the baby?" Richard asked.

"Partly. But I can't imagine her holding out much longer. She's strong, but she's sensible too."

"I don't know. Karen seemed just as determined as before in there," Richard pointed out. "Can't you talk her into dropping the charges against Alien?"

"I don't know," Sid said slowly.

"Will you at least try?"

He nodded. "Sure, Richard. For you."

"Hey, this isn't just for me, you know. It's for the whole cul-de-sac—for Knots Landing."

"Yeah?" Sid questioned. "I haven't heard anyone else complaining. Just you."

They continued to stare at each other.

"I'll do what I can, Richard." Sid dropped his gaze. "And by the way, you're not worth a damn when it comes to adjusting timing."

Richard chuckled.

"Why'd Mom get so mad out there?" Eric asked as he and his brother changed into clean clothing in their bedroom.

"I don't know," Michael said. "Maybe it's the baby."

"I dunno. I think it's the bikers."

"She's not afraid of them," Michael insisted. "She's not afraid of anything."

"Ha, ha," his brother teased. "Dad, maybe, but not Mom."

Eric pulled the clean blue shirt over his head and smoothed it down on his chest.

"Do you think they'll hurt her?" Michael's young face appeared older with fear.

Eric looked at him for a moment. His back stiffened. His eyes glowed, and his hand wavered before him. "I am Mysto the Wizard. I will *hyp-no-tize* you!"

"Stop it," Michael said, kicking his brother's legs.

"Mysto!" Eric thrust his hands outward like the Frankenstein monster as he stomped toward Michael.

"Come on, knock it off!" Michael moved away. "That doesn't scare me like it did when I was a little kid. Do you think they'll hurt Mom? Do you?"

Eric snorted and he leaned against the bedroom wall. Stuffing his hands into his pockets, he muttered, "I don't know. I don't know. How should I know?"

"I hope not," Michael said solemnly.

Eric hit the wall with his knee. "Don't worry about it. Worry about getting another brother or sister. *That* would be a major problem."

"Why should I worry about something like that?" Michael lifted his shoulders so they almost touched his ears. "She'll either have it or she won't. I hope she does have it, because— well, the other way isn't good." Michael's face screwed up with concentration.

Eric whistled through his teeth. "Yeah, I guess so. I just don't want some screaming kid in here before the end of the year. I don't want to have to live with a little brat just like you were."

Michael grimaced as he poked ten fingers into his brother's midsection.

"Hey!" Eric cried out, surprised by the sudden attack. "Leave me alone! Besides, that's what I do to you. You can't do it to me!"

"I can now," Michael grinned. "I'm getting older." He paused. "You know, sometimes when I'm eating dinner or something I see Mom staring at me funny. You know? Like she's thinking about me."

111

Eric nodded. "I've seen her do that to me too."

"What's going on?"

"I don't know."

The door burst open. "Would you *children* be quiet?" Diana demanded as she stormed into the room.

"Not for you," Eric answered.

"I'm trying to memorize my lines for the play, and it sounds like a freeway in here."

"Dumb play," Michael chided.

Diana pointed her finger at him. "When you grow up maybe you'll finally appreciate good drama."

"Boy, what's wrong with her?" Michael asked Eric in a loud stage whisper.

"She thinks she's real grown up. Overnight." Eric made a mocking face and then turned to stare at his sister.

"I am—almost," Diana said smugly. "More than you know."

"Oh, brother!" Eric rolled his eyes.

"Anyway—what were you guys yelling about in here while I was trying to study?"

"Mom's baby," Eric said.

Diana's feisty look faded. Her eyes narrowed.

"You don't like Mom's baby," Michael observed.

"I don't like the idea of it." Diana held the back of her neck with her hand. "Yeah. That's right, I don't!"

"You're just jealous."

"I am not, Eric!" Diana snapped. "I just hope she does the right thing. The *only* thing she can do."

"What's that?" the boys asked in unison.

"Have the baby," Diana said simply.

"Really?" Michael knit his brow in confusion. "I thought you didn't want her to have a baby."

"I don't, but the alternative's worse. All she can do right now is have the baby. It's too late for anything else."

"That's not what Daddy said."

Diana turned and walked to the door. "Just be quiet and let me learn my lines."

"Did you get the part?"

"Not yet." Diana shivered dramatically. "But I'm practicing just in case."

"Buzzy Marek!" Michael sang. "You love Buzzy Marek!"

Diana's face flushed. "Where'd you hear that?"

"Everyone knows," Eric goaded her.

"That's not true!" Diana stamped her foot as she said the words.

"Come on, you might as well admit it."

"Just keep it down in here," she fretted, and turned to leave.

The boys grinned, then started a whooping free-for-all.

"You're sure you're okay, Val?" Gary stood in his living room, straightening his tie.

"I think so. But Gary, it was horrible! Those girls chasing us on their motorcycles. It gave me such a fright I had to shut my eyes to get through it."

Gary wrapped an arm around her waist and squeezed. "I'm sorry, honey. I thought we'd left all that behind us."

"Gary, sometimes I wish—"

"Wish what?" he asked. "You're not going to start that again, honey, are you?" His voice was mild.

"I don't know. Knots Landing's such a—a—different place. So different from Texas. I don't feel at home here yet."

"That'll come with time," Gary promised.

Val gave him a weak smile. "I know it will. And this motorcycle gang'll have to leave sometime. Things'll get back to normal."

"That's right." He kissed her swiftly. "Gotta get back to work."

"Knots Landing Motors can't get by without you?" Val asked, looking at him hopefully.

"Don't think so. Sorry, honey."

Val pouted. "Oh, all right. I thought we might get to—to—"

"Tonight." He winked, kissed her cheek, and left.

Val stood at the door, watching her husband walk to the car, and then she wandered into the kitchen.

"Good work, girls," Music said as they sat on a cliff overlooking the ocean.

"That bitch sure was scared!" Mary said cheerfully. "She couldn't even look at me!"

"It was fun while it lasted," Alison laughed.

"Yeah, until that damned police car showed." Mary spat on the ground. "We had to clear out."

"It doesn't matter," Music said. "You lost him."

"Right."

"And you scared the Fairgate broad. Good—things are going fine."

"What's next?" Mary inquired. "And can I do it, whatever it is?"

Music gave her a wry grin. "You're a greedy woman, Mary."

"Yeah, don't I know it," Alison added.

Mary shot her a stinging look. "Hey, sister, no one's forcing you to ride with us," she said haughtily. "If you don't like the company, buzz off." Mary turned to Music. "Could we go off somewhere together?"

"Now?" Music asked.

"Sure. We could have some fun." Mary leaned over to whisper in his ear. "I need you."

Music stepped back. "Not now, Mary. I got some thinkin' to do."

She sighed. "About what?"

Music looked at her quickly. "About Alien, man! He's still in there rotting in that cell, and we have to come up with some plan to get him out."

"Yeah, I know." Mary's manner became petulant.

"Hey, no one's forcing you to help out," Alison huffed to the woman.

Mary turned to her and laughed.

"Girls, girls, no cat fights," Music warned.

"I am not a girl!" Mary chafed. "I'm a woman, damn you!"

"Mary, Alison, get lost. I'm tired of your whining and your nagging. I have to think."

Mary shrugged and walked off. After she was gone Alison approached Music.

"What the hell do you want, man?" he asked, annoyed.

"Nothing, Music. I was just wondering if you've seen Ross."

"Not lately," he said. "He rode off an hour ago to buy some beer and I ain't seen him since."

"Okay," she said thinly, and headed back toward the road.

Music sat, figuring and planning, as he watched the waves below him.

Chapter Ten

Karen Decides

Karen sat slumped on the couch in her living room listening to Sid putter around in the kitchen as he fixed a snack.

"I just can't do it," she mumbled.

"What's that, honey?" Sid yelled from the kitchen.

"I can't drop the charges. It's against everything I believe in. I can't let a criminal go free just because a few of his friends are harassing the neighborhood. What would that make me?" Karen fingered the neck of her blouse.

"I didn't hear that, Karen," Sid said.

She sighed. "If I could be sure that they won't go any further, that no one would get hurt . . . there wouldn't be any decision to make. But they might be rough enough to try something worse— and I can't expose my family and friends to violent attacks."

Her husband entered from the kitchen holding a sandwich. "What were you saying?"

"I'm trying to figure out whether I can drop the charge against Alien or not."

Sid's face brightened momentarily, then quickly returned to a careful neutral expression. "And?" He bit into the sandwich.

"And . . . I don't know." Karen folded her hands. "Sid, you don't think they'll actually try to hurt us, do you? I mean, physically?"

"I don't know." His words were garbled by bread and turkey. "They do look tough."

"Yes, and that's what scares me. I could never forgive myself if anything happened to anyone."

Sid nodded, eyes half-closed, chewing thoughtfully.

Karen's eyes widened and her lips parted. "Sid, if I do drop the charge, the gang will move out of Knots Landing, won't they?"

He shrugged noncommittally and wiped a splotch of mayonnaise from his upper lip. "It's anyone's guess, but it seems likely."

"It would be worth it to have a safe beach and neighborhood again." She stretched. "I'm exhausted and it's only afternoon. This is so draining for me, Sid."

"It's draining all of us, but not as much as you." Another corner of the sandwich disappeared into his mouth.

She gazed at him. "Yes, I suppose it is. Sid, what do you think I should do?"

He swallowed. "All I know is this sandwich needs more mayonnaise." He went back into the kitchen.

"Thanks for all your help," Karen said sarcastically.

"You're welcome."

She sat mulling over the problem for several minutes until Sid buzzed into the living room pulling on his coat. "Gotta go back to work, honey." He bent and kissed her cheek. "You know that whatever you decide, I'll support you." He hurried to the front door and was gone.

Karen reached for the phone, retracted her hand, but then lifted the receiver and decisively dialed. Richard should be back at his office by now, Karen thought. He'd better be—she needed to tell him before she changed her mind.

A connection was made.

"Listen, Richard, I've decided . . ." Karen blurted out before he could even say hello.

"Karen?" he asked.

"Yes. I want to drop the charge against Alien," she said. A moment of silence followed her words.

"Richard? Are you there?"

"Yeah, yeah I'm here. Karen, that's wonderful. Where are you right now?"

"At home."

"Why don't you meet me at the police station in, say, fifteen minutes?" Richard did not want Karen to reconsider.

"I'll be there. And thanks, Richard."

"Thank *you*. I'll see you soon." He rang off.

Karen hung up and headed for her station wagon.

Thirty minutes later, Karen walked down the front steps of the police station with Richard.

"You surprised me in there," he said. "I'm glad that you decided to make the right decision."

"Don't think I didn't have second thoughts,"

Karen said, her face pinched. "I'm not sure I did the right thing. But I don't want anyone hurt because of me." She glanced at him quickly. "Thanks for helping me out, Richard."

"No problem," he assured her. "That's what lawyers are for. But I wish I could convince you that it was the right thing to do."

"Richard, it was the *easiest* thing to do, considering the situation. That doesn't make it right." Karen's look was still pained.

He smiled. "Karen, I'm a lawyer. I know how the law works. Even if you hadn't dropped the charge not much would have happened to Alien. Maybe thirty days or so in jail."

Karen's jaw dropped. "That's all?" She was stunned.

He nodded. "He didn't intentionally hurt Michael."

"But he—"

Richard interrupted. "Yes, he hit him, but technically the incident would be classified as an accident."

"That was no accident," she said, seething as they turned toward the parking lot.

"Alien could have been fined too."

Karen frowned. "You still haven't convinced me, but I've done it so there's no sense worrying now."

"Besides, Karen, no matter what—you couldn't have won."

She looked at him. "No?"

"Sure, he might have been sentenced and fined, maybe locked up for a while longer, but he would have gotten even. If he had been fined, how do you suppose he'd pay it?"

"I don't know." Karen's voice was dull with defeat. They stopped on the corner.

"Alien would have had to rely on his friends to raise the money. They have some sure-fire methods—armed robbery, selling dope to kids—"

"Enough," Karen cut him off.

"Listen, when you consider everything, the damage they've done to all of us, including your son—and the damage they could do in the near future—it was the only move you could make."

"I know," Karen said. "But that doesn't make it the right thing to do."

"From a practical viewpoint—" Richard began.

"Practical? Who's being practical?"

"From a practical viewpoint, it was the right tactic. Take my word for it." Richard was using his best courtroom voice.

"I hope I don't regret this in the morning." Her voice was already heavy with remorse.

They turned the corner. Karen gasped as she saw Music heading down the sidewalk toward them.

"Easy, Karen," Richard said, and gripped her shoulder.

Karen shrugged it off. "Let me do the talking."

"What a pleasant surprise," Music said.

"Oh, really? For whom?" Karen's tone was cutting.

Music didn't seem to notice. "I'm just on my way to visit my friend Alien." He turned and looked at the police station. "He don't like being locked up in there. It's driving him crazy, really messing up his mind. And he didn't have much left to mess up."

"Really?" Karen said derisively. "He doesn't like that awful place?" She became deadly serious. "He should have thought about that before he hurt my son."

"Hey, hey." Music lifted his hands as if to fight off invisible foes. "Bad karma, man. I know he'd really appreciate it if you'll let him out of there."

"Karen," Richard began, "I think we should—"

Karen glanced at him sharply. "Shut up, Richard."

"Been having any trouble in the neighborhood lately?" Music asked, his eyes twinkling.

"You pig!" Karen exploded. "As if you didn't know! Your buddies have been having some fun at our expense!"

"Hey, like I said, they're animals." Music's face darkened, "Wild. Uncontrollable. And you've got their leader locked up in there!" He slapped his open hand against the white block wall of the station. "Are you going to let him go or not, lady?" His eyes were red-veined, furious.

Karen stood firm, poised to offer a wrathful response, but her anger seemed to paralyze her throat.

Before Karen could say more, Richard stepped forward. "She already has. They're giving him back his stuff in there."

"You're kidding me." Music jerked his head back as if in shock. "She dropped the charge?"

"Yes," Richard said. He looked at Karen. "Let's get out of here." He put his arm around her shoulders.

"Your friends are *very* persuasive," Karen said, finding words. "Tell them I've done my part. Now I wish you'd all leave Knots Landing.

Now. Today!''

Music bit his lip. ''Sure thing,'' he said, his voice too confident, too loud. ''Just remember, I didn't have nothing to do with what happened to your neighborhood. Okay? It was the other guys. I just hang around with them. Alien's their leader. You got that straight?''

''Sure, I got it straight,'' Richard said in a mocking imitation of Music's voice. ''Why don't you go see your friend?'' He stood a good inch shorter than Music, but he straightened his shoulders as he faced the biker.

''Sure, it's way cool.'' Music shrugged, then turned toward the front entrance.

''He's got a lot of nerve.'' Karen continued to smolder as they went on to the parking lot. ''Expecting me to believe him.''

''Calm down,'' Richard said. ''It's over. You've finished it now. Life'll get back to normal in Knots Landing, and Laura will have my dinner ready for me every night.''

Karen shook her head. ''I wish I could believe that it's over, but I didn't like the look in Music's eyes when he said the gang would leave Knots Landing. How can I trust him?''

''You can't,'' Richard said bluntly. ''But you can hope for the best.''

Karen opened her car door and waved to Richard as he walked to his vehicle, trying to erase the image of Music's face from her mind.

''Man, what took you so long?'' Alien said, bounding down the front steps of the station toward his friend, his shoulder-length hair flapping in the wind.

"Hey, man, twenty-four hours ain't that long." Music smiled. "You make it sound like you've been in that hole for years."

"Seemed like it." Alien shuddered. "Where's the gang?"

"Not far. Come on." Music walked toward his bike.

"Everyone ready to move on?" Alien asked.

"No. Why?"

"Hell, I'm more than ready to get outa here. I never want to see this town or that building again."

They halted before Music's motorcycle. "It looks pretty good. She scratched it when she knocked it over, didn't she?"

"Yeah," Music said slowly.

"How's my bike?"

"Running," Music replied, and half smiled.

Alien grabbed Music's shoulders and shook him. "Come on, man, how's it look?" His breath puffed against Music's forehead.

"Not bad," he said. "Busted headlight—"

"Damn!"

"A couple scratches, that's about all." Music looked at his friend and raised his eyebrows. "You still wanna move on?"

Alien was silent, staring at the long scar on Music's fuel tank. "I dunno," he mused. "I dunno now."

"Maybe we shouldn't leave right away, Alien."

"But the guys are waiting for us in Laguna," he considered.

"Yeah, and the dudes can just wait longer. It won't kill them ."

Alien tightened his lips, still focusing on the damaged bike.

"That lady kept you locked up a night and a day, man." Music moved closer to his buddy. "She did that to you, Alien. You haven't been locked up for ten years."

"Yeah."

"Are you gonna let her get away with that?"

The big biker finally looked up from the fuel tank. "Hell no!"

"She's gotta pay for that, don't she?"

"Yeah," he agreed. "How?"

"I'll think of something. We're pretty smart, man. I got you outa jail, didn't I?"

"Yeah. Hey Music, what'd you do to her?"

The biker laughed. "Man, do I have some stories for you!"

Music straddled the bike and kicked it into life. Alien slid onto the seat behind him and reached down to grasp the license plate for stability.

Music turned back toward Alien. "If we're gonna get even, we've got to do it quick and then get out."

"But I thought the cops were a joke in this town," Alien said.

"They are, but they might get lucky."

"Not with us, buddy," Alien shouted into Music's ear as the biker gunned the engine. "Hey, I can handle six cop cars and a pack of sniffer-dogs," Alien boasted. "We're safe as long as we stick to the countryside and the cliffs."

"Maybe we should lay low for a day or two, make them think we've left."

"Yeah," Alien said, enjoying the idea.

"She has a daughter," Music suggested. "The Fairgate broad."

"How old?" Alien asked.

Music shrugged. "Must be fifteen, sixteen. She's a real fox. Remember, the real cute one on the beach? I've had Ross watching her go to school."

"So? So what do we do?" Alien asked.

Music shifted and zipped out onto the street. He turned back toward Alien and shouted: "You was looking for a good way to get back at that broad, right?"

"Yeah."

"I just thought her daughter might be it."

Alien licked his lips. "She's old enough," he drawled and laughed harshly.

"What do you think we should do with her?"

"I don't know. Snatch her or something. Make her mother sweat it out a little."

Music shook his head and pointed to his ear. The wind and combined noises of the cars they passed blocked out the man's words.

The biker squeezed the gas, racing the engine, speeding his bike toward the gang's hangout high above the restless ocean.

Chapter Eleven
Childhood Relic

"I think it'll be fun," Michael said to his brother as they stood in the kitchen.

"Sure," Diana said sarcastically. "You said the same thing about Rusty, remember?"

"That was different. Rusty was a dog," Michael pointed out.

"Dog, goldfish, baby—it's all the same thing, Michael."

"You're crazy, Diana. You don't even know the difference between a baby and a dog."

"They all sound like a great idea until you've had to take care of them for a month." Diana frowned.

"What? You think you're going to take care of the baby?" Eric asked, making saucer eyes at Michael.

"Sure."

"Mom's going to take care of it, Diana. We won't have to," Eric insisted.

"Wanna bet?" Diana asked, half-smiling.

"How many times have I been stuck with you two?"

Sid Fairgate walked into the kitchen. "What's going on in here?" He perused his three children. "Looks like a huddle."

"We're talking about the baby," Diana said testily. "I'm telling them how it'll change our lives."

"I think it'll be great," Michael said.

"You're the one who's crazy, Michael."

"Diana, you're just worried someone else'll get more attention than you do." Michael tapped her shoulder.

"I am not!" she hissed.

"Yes you are!"

"Eric, stay out of this!"

"Hey, hey, calm down everybody!" Sid motioned downward with his hands.

"I'm just trying to be realistic." Diana put her hands on her hips. "*Someone* has to be." She glanced warily at her father.

Sid crossed his arms. "Look, I'm glad you're talking about the baby. But we might be jumping the gun."

The kids all wore confused expressions. Sid cleared his throat and took a deep breath.

"Kids," he said as he exhaled slowly. "Stick around. Your mother still has a big decision to make ahead of her."

"A decision?" Michael asked.

"Yes. She hasn't made up her mind yet."

"But she's already pregnant, isn't she?" Michael's voice was pitched high with concern.

Diana looked at her father, eyes intense. "You don't mean—you don't mean she's thinking about having an abortion, do you?''

The silence became heavy. Sid nodded.

"I don't believe it!" Diana scowled.

"I didn't think you liked the idea of another baby, Diana," Sid reminded her gently.

"I don't, Dad, but she *can't* have an abortion!"

"*I* like the idea of a baby," Michael piped up.

"Me too, kind of." Eric brushed his thick hair out of his eyes. "It's better than the other way."

Diana stood before her father. "Daddy, you can't let her do this! Talk to her. Convince her just to have the baby and—and not try to undc what's been done!"

Sid reached out for her hand. "I know how you feel, honey. I don't care much for the idea myself."

"Well then?" Diana asked.

He smiled faintly and moved his attention from one child to the next. "I hope she decides to keep the baby, but I also love your mother . . . very much. And I want her to be happy. Can you understand that? I think we all want her to be happy."

Eric and Michael nodded slowly, but continued to appear puzzled. Diana sighed and lifted an eyebrow.

"Right now she's not too happy. Your mother's upset and confused. She doesn't know her next move, and she's more than a little scared. She needs us now more than ever before. I want all of us to make things as easy as possible for her."

"What can we do?" Diana asked quietly.

"Lots. Let her know that we love her—and support her. That we're trying to understand."

"I don't know if I do, Dad," Michael said.

"Me neither," his brother added.

"I don't think any of us do, Michael. But let's give it a good try, okay? She really needs us right now and we've got to be there to help her."

His children nodded thoughtfully.

"Good. We'll talk again later. I'll keep you up on any decisions she makes, if she doesn't tell you herself."

"Okay," Diana murmured as she exhaled loudly.

Upstairs, Karen Fairgate lay stretched full-length on the bed, dressed in her housecoat. She stared at the ceiling, wishing for a few minutes of midday sleep.

She should be doing the laundry but the prospect of load after load of clothing, measuring detergent, and stuffing things from one machine into another wasn't too attractive. Besides, she had much too much on her mind.

Karen closed her eyes and tried to relax herself further, then opened them. Pushing over onto her left shoulder, Karen laid her face on her hand and shut her eyes again.

No luck. Karen groaned, swung her legs off the bed and rose from it. She wouldn't get any rest that afternoon. She stopped before the dresser mirror, looked at her reflection, and then quickly away from it down to the bureau. What a mess, she thought.

She straightened out the jars and atomizers there, wiped up a patch of spilled make-up with a tissue, then smoothed out the bedspread and walked out of the bedroom.

Karen moved toward the stairs, trying to wrench thoughts of the baby from her mind. As she passed Michael and Eric's room she glanced in through the door, then stopped suddenly, peering inside.

The room was heaped with artifacts of childhood: tangled pairs of soiled jeans and socks, Frisbees, partially-built submarine models, records, mitts and baseballs, two pairs of skates, torn comic books, a cracked bat, more clothing, a skateboard, apple cores, and a welter of other toys and apparel. The beds were jumbled masses of blankets and sheets.

Karen almost smiled. "What's new?" she said aloud. Another messy room. So what—she'd seen a million of them.

She started into the room, then stepped back out from the doorway. "Not today," she decided. She wasn't going to clean that dirty room today. It was Michael and Eric's mess—let them clean it up.

After all, if she was going to have another baby, things would have to change. The boys would have to learn to pick up after themselves. *If* she was going to have another one, Karen emphasized to herself.

She closed the door, hesitated, and then opened it. Surveying the damage again, she chuckled softly.

I can't be upset at them for being kids, Karen thought as she walked into the room and stood among the ruins. "First, the clothing." Karen quickly made the beds and then retrieved every article of wearing apparel within sight. Socks turned up under the mattresses, behind the door, buried in the depths of the closet.

Next, she threw jelly-stained shirts and grass-stained pants into a pile with the rest of their clothing. She then gathered it up into her arms and hauled it out to the washing machine, where she knew she'd eventually have to tackle getting it all clean.

That done, she returned to the room and began rounding up the assorted foodstuff and potato chip bags that littered the floor. While she worked Karen tried to keep her thoughts away from the new baby. She poured her concentration into her activities.

Karen found one particularly large piece of paper lodged behind the dresser. She tugged at it for half a minute before standing up and dragging the dresser away from the wall.

When she bent to pull the paper from its hiding place, Karen's face flushed and her heart melted. In her hands she held a faded Christmas card she'd received from Michael years ago. She'd thought it had been thrown away.

Karen blinked as she gazed at it. On the pale red construction paper, in Michael's schoolboy scrawl, were cartoon representations of the entire Fairgate family, with their respective names below them in careful block letters. Behind the family a Christmas tree sparkled in Crayola splendor, while beneath it dozens of presents crowded the trunk. Above the scene ran the inscription: "Peace and Goodwill, from the Fairgate Family."

Karen sat down on the dusty floor, cradling the picture gingerly, as if it were a fragile relic from a long-lost age. Years of memories flooded through her. The moment when she first realized she was pregnant with Diana; the labors and deliveries of her three children; taking Eric home from the hospital for the first time; all those screaming haircut sessions; bathing Michael in a tiny tub which the boy could now wear like a hat on his head; the first steps and words her children had managed.

That was all years ago now. Diana was sixteen, and Michael and Eric were growing up quickly. Within a few years all three of her children probably would be living away from home.

Karen set the card on her lap and continued to gaze at it, her eyes red and misty. She had liked those years. No—she had *loved* them! She'd been able to raise three children and not be chained to her house. She'd fashioned three reasonably well-adjusted people who were on the verge of breaking away, to start fresh, independent lives.

She touched the face of the card, then moved her finger against the brittle waxy lines. Her finger tingled. Maybe having a baby wouldn't be so bad, Karen thought. She'd certainly enjoyed it the first three times around. But that was part of the dilemma: she thought she'd left those years behind her.

Karen had been laying plans for her life alone with Sid when their children had moved from home. She had envisioned an exciting, challenging future, filled with new possibilities and experiences. A baby would alter her life irrevocably. But was that so bad?

Karen sighed. If she couldn't make up her mind and waited too long, there wouldn't be anything she could do anyway. Even if she wanted to at that point!

No. That wasn't good enough. She had to *want* the baby or she couldn't see having it at all. It wouldn't be fair to her or to the child.

She closed her eyes, rubbed them, and tried to still her mind. She held the card lightly on her lap as her thoughts raced on, despite her efforts to halt them. Sounds from downstairs roused her after a few moments. Karen shook her head gently in another attempt to clear her many concerns, and then she smiled.

It was the right decision, she told herself—the only decision she could make.

"Whadja think so far?" Music asked, as he sat with Alien and Ross at their campsite.

The sun hung low on the western horizon. The air was brisk—night would be cool from the moist sea breezes flowing up from the beach and over the cliffs.

"Sounds okay to me," Alien said. "But what do we do with the broad once we have her?"

"I can think of a few things," Ross smirked, his eyes gleaming.

"I bet you can," Music said, "but leave that to me. It'll be something to remember." He grinned.

"When do we do it?"

"I don't know, Ross. Soon."

"When?" Alien whined, grabbing Music's shoulder.

"Take it easy, buddy," he cautioned him. "You're too tense. Keep that up and you'll go to an early grave."

"Come on, Music, when?" Alien puffed his

breath in short spurts as he stared at Music.

The man thought for a moment, squinting his eyes into slits. "How about tonight?" he suggested. "That too early for you, Alien? You wanna think about it?"

The biker's bearded face brightened. "Yeah. I mean, I like that. We grab the broad tonight."

Music laughed. "I didn't think there'd be any objections. Let's get ready."

Alien's eyes darted back and forth as he thought of the night's adventures, and, as they moved, they reflected the flaming rays of the color-charged, setting sun.

Karen walked down the stairs. She'd changed into a pair of white pants and a blue blouse, and had touched up her hair in the mirror before leaving her bedroom.

"This calls for a celebration," she said.

Sid looked up from the magazine he was leafing through, while Eric and Michael lifted their eyes from the model they were working on.

"What kind of celebration?" Diana said pleasantly as she sipped a glass of water, reading the script on the couch.

"Yeah, honey, what's up?" Sid asked.

"What do you think?" Karen smiled broadly.

"You're having the baby?" Sid dropped the magazine onto the floor and stood.

"Yes," she exclaimed.

"Sweetheart, that's wonderful!" Sid kissed her hard on the mouth.

"Hey! It's more than wonderful!" Michael jumped up.

"I think so too." Karen looked lovingly at her

children. "Thanks, all of you."

"For what?" Eric asked.

"For helping me make this decision. I couldn't have done it without you."

"But we didn't do anything, Mom." Michael had walked over to his mother.

"Yes, you did," she said gently, and touched his forehead. "All of you." She moved her gaze to include Eric and Diana.

"Can you tell us about it, honey?" Sid's face was radiant with happiness.

Karen began. "When I found out I was pregnant, I couldn't believe it. I started thinking things like: I'm a grown woman—I've already got three wonderful, healthy, perfectly normal children—who wants another one?" She hugged her shoulders briefly. "That was my head at work, and I listened to it for a while. But in my *heart* I knew the answer all the time. I want another baby." She paused, smiling. "I want this fourth child because of the three I've already got."

The kids looked at each other, wondering what their mother was trying to say.

"I don't get it, Mom," Eric said.

"I'm sorry, Eric," Karen apologized. "I'm not making myself clear. Maybe I can give you examples." She looked at her daughter. "Diana, you know the way you just burst out and tell it like it is?"

She tilted her head to one side. "Sure."

"And you, Eric," she said, focusing on her elder son. "You're so suave and self-assured—most of the time, but not always."

Eric looked down, embarrassed. "I guess."

"And Michael, my little innocent." She touched the bandage on his head. "You remind me of things I hope I never lose."

The boy was quiet, but didn't look down.

"Do you see what I'm saying? I look at you kids and I see little bits of me, and then I watch myself and see parts of you." Karen glanced at her husband and flushed at seeing the emotion on his face. "If I didn't have this child I'd never stop thinking about all the things I'd miss—and I'd miss so much. I know, because I've got you three." She waited. "So that's why I said thank you."

Sid gazed at her, his eyes soft with love. Eric and Michael sat looking at her honestly, openly, while Diana smiled nervously on the couch.

"So let's celebrate!" Karen said brightly.

Sid embraced her.

"What do you want to do?" Diana asked.

"Go out to eat?" Sid suggested. "Hey, we could go to that fancy place that just opened."

"No," Karen said. "Let's just stay at home and enjoy the evening—together."

"Sounds good to me," Sid agreed. "I'll be close to you."

"Oh, brother!" Michael grimaced. "All this lovey-dovey stuff!"

His parents laughed.

Later, Diana found her mother in the kitchen. "Mom . . . " she began.

"Come here, you."

Diana crossed the kitchen quickly and Karen pulled her daughter into a tight hug. After a minute, Diana moved back and looked squarely at her mother.

"I've been pretty dumb about this whole thing," she lamented.

"It hasn't been easy for any of us. You're no worse than I've been." Karen smoothed Diana's hair.

"I guess I didn't like the idea of sharing you with somebody else," Diana confessed, then looked down. "I didn't realize it, I guess."

Karen laughed. "Really? That's funny. I had the same feeling."

"You did?" Diana's eyes were wide with wonder.

"Sure. I was uneasy about sharing *me* with someone else. But then, I figure that if we handle this right, there'll be lots left over for everyone. Okay?"

Diana moved her head up and down vigorously. "Okay!" She turned to leave the kitchen.

"Oh, Diana—I'm kind of hoping for a girl. What about you?"

She looked back, grinning. "*Definitely* a girl."

Karen returned the grin as Diana blew her a kiss and walked out of sight.

Chapter Twelve

Kidnap

Gary Ewing dipped the last piece of chicken into the batter and slid it into the skillet. The chicken fried fragrantly, its aroma wafting across the kitchen to Val, who stood punching out biscuits from a thick white dough.

"A baby in the cul-de-sac," Val said. "Isn't that kind of exciting?"

"Sure is." Gary studied the chicken. "You ever noticed the way people's heads turn when a pregnant woman walks by?"

Val nodded. "I remember. They treat them— special. It's a special time for a woman."

"For a man, too," Gary said.

They glanced at each other, the chicken and biscuits momentarily forgotten. Val's eyes were searching, hopeful, while Gary's were interested but noncommittal.

A second later they returned to their cooking. Gary enjoyed watching the poultry turn golden brown, the oil crackling and sputtering around it.

"It's the only thing that two people can really share," Val observed. "It's not like a house or a car or something you buy. It's something that two people—well, *create*."

"Yeah," Gary replied. "It kinda fills a space where you didn't even realize there *was* a space."

They were silent for a moment. Val punched out another biscuit while Gary removed a drumstick from the skillet.

"Gary," Val began. "Have you thought any more about . . . you know . . . well, having . . ."

He laughed shortly. "You mean having another baby?"

Val looked down. "Yeah."

"Sure I have," he said. "We've got that extra room upstairs. It's perfectly good, but it's doing nothing except gathering dust. Maybe we could put it to good use."

Valene set the biscuits aside. "Really?" Her eyes were wide.

"Sure. Why not?" Gary's mouth curled up at the corners.

"It's been such a long time, Gary. It's kind of scary to think about it."

Gary nodded. "I'll admit it, it is. But we've got plenty of time to decide."

Val stared at him. "I've got so many ideas for that room," she declared, then blushed. "Listen to me! I'm talking like we're gonna have one!"

"Yeah, but you're just talking," Gary said. "No harm in that." He turned another leg.

Valene smiled. "What do you think about pink curtains in the nursery?"

Gary made a mock frown. "Absolutely not!"

"Why not?"

He shrugged. "Well . . . blue would be better for a boy."

"Gary!" Val's eyes sparkled.

He laughed. "Just talk," he said

His wife looked down at her work. "How many biscuits was I needin'?"

A splotch of hot oil splattered from the skillet, striking Gary's right arm.

"Damn!" he shouted, backing away from the stove. "It burned me again." He rubbed the red spot on his arm and turned to Val. "Honey," he said.

"What, Gary?" Val counted the biscuits she'd already made, then looked at the dough and estimated the number of biscuits she could produce from it.

"Do you want to try to have a baby?" he asked.

She looked up at him, her face glowed, but the smile trembled on her lips. "Sure I do, honey," Val said.

"Then what's wrong? I can see it on your face," Gary sounded bewildered. He removed the last of the chicken from the pan and turned off the heat.

"I don't know," she answered in a hushed voice. "I'm a little scared at the thought."

Gary wiped his hands on the apron tied around his waist. "Yeah, I guess I know how you feel." He went to her and kissed her cheek, then wrapped his arms around her waist. "Better finish getting dinner ready," he said. "I have to go over the new advertising campaign with Sid tonight."

"Okay, honey," Val returned to her biscuits,

her expression solemn. As she worked on, though, she found herself smiling.

The Fairgate family filtered out of the dining room, Sid and Karen moving with their coffee cups to the living room, the kids quickly scattering throughout the house. Sid and Karen were alone.

The doorbell rang just as Karen sat down on the couch. She started to rise, but Sid moved more quickly.

"Don't get up," he insisted, smiling, and walked to the door. Sid opened it. "Hi, Gary, Val," he said, stepping back to let them in.

"Hi. Finished with dinner?" Val asked.

"Just done," Karen said. "Come on in."

Sid closed the door behind them.

"Can we get you some coffee?" Karen stood up.

Gary sat in the chair, holding a large manila envelope. "We'd love some."

Karen went to the kitchen and in a moment returned with two cups, which she handed to the Ewings.

"Thanks," Gary took a burning sip. "Good coffee."

"I sure do like the way all those tires got changed on our cars so fast," Val said.

"That's one of the advantages of being a car dealer—you can replace twelve slashed tires with twelve brand-new steel belted radials on a moment's notice," Gary observed.

Sid took a long swallow of coffee. "I just hope we won't have to do that again."

"Don't even think like that!" Karen sputtered.

"I agree," Gary added. "I don't think those guys'll be doing us any more harm. They're probably long gone by now."

"I wish I could believe that," Sid said reluctantly. "It's just that I have this feeling that we're—well, that we're not completely *safe* yet."

As if on cue, the rip of a motorcycle blazed in through the opened front windows.

"Damn!" Sid jumped up, sloshing his coffee onto the carpet. He swiftly made his way to the front door. He whipped it open and ran outside.

A motorcycle cop pulled up in front of his house and stopped.

"Everything okay, Mr. Fairgate?" the man asked politely as Sid rushed up to him.

Sid slammed a fist into his hand. "Yeah, fine. Thanks, officer." Sid's heart was pounding.

The cop waved and drove off into the darkness.

Sid returned to his house, closed the door hard and walked into the living room. Val knelt beside the spill, busily blotting it with a napkin.

"Leave it, Val," Karen said, her eyes fixed on Sid's perspiring face. "It needs to be cleaned anyway."

Val rose. "I'll get Sid some more coffee."

"Thanks, Val, but I'm jumpy enough as it is. I'm just not so sure it's over." Sid sat and gripped the chair's arms, his knuckles pale.

Eric ambled down the stairs, jostling a load of books under his arm.

"See you later," he said, otherwise dismissing the adults on his way out.

"Where're you going?" Sid inquired.

"Over to Joe's to study," he replied quickly.

143

"Study alone tonight."

"Dad, it's just around the corner!" Eric pleaded.

"Eric!" Karen's voice was sharp.

The boy huffed. "Oh, okay," he grumbled, and headed back upstairs. "But I thought the crisis was over," he added.

"It is over," Karen asserted. "But we want things quiet tonight."

"Then how come Dad just said—"

"Never mind, Eric. Just go study upstairs."

Visibly unhappy, the boy looked at his mother. "All right, all right." He disappeared at the top of the stairs.

"Want to go over that copy now, Sid?" Gary asked, and opened the envelope he had been holding. He took out some typewritten pages and handed them to Sid.

"Copy?" Sid stared at the papers.

"The advertising copy. The reason we're here—remember, I mentioned it to you this afternoon?"

Sid nodded and scanned the pages but couldn't seem to concentrate. He shrugged and handed them back to Gary. "You take care of it, Gary. From now on you're in charge of advertising for Knots Landing Motors."

Gary looked pleased and stuffed the pages back into the envelope. He turned to Val and Karen. "The advertising guy wants Sid to make his own commercials."

"You mean like that other fella on TV who does the ads for his own shoe store?" Val asked.

"Right!" Gary warmed to the subject. "In the first one he wants Sid to sky-dive from a balloon, right down onto the dealership's lot."

Karen giggled. "I can't imagine Sid doing something like that." She was about to tease Sid, but stopped when she saw the worried expression on his face.

"Hi," Diana said, walking down the stairs. "Doing something like what?"

"Skydiving from a balloon." Karen giggled again despite herself.

"What!"

"You're not going anywhere tonight," Sid suddenly interjected.

"But I haven't even asked you—"

"I don't care," Sid commanded. "Not tonight." His voice was strangely abrasive.

"But I've got to go to rehearsal," Diana argued.

"No." Sid's mouth was tight.

"Daddy!" Diana cried. "How can you—"

"I'm sorry, honey," Karen interrupted. "Did you get the part?"

"Yes." Diana was barely audible, her voice flat.

"That's wonderful!" Val smiled.

"I guess."

"Ah. Not the second lead, maybe?" Karen guessed.

"No. The *first* lead."

"Oh, I'm sorry."

"Sorry?" Gary asked. "Are we missing something here?"

"It's a long story," Karen said, in a voice that discouraged any more questions.

Sid shook his head. "Long or short, the rehearsal's cancelled tonight. For you, anyway."

"Daddy, you can't! They'll replace me if I don't show up tonight!"

"Sid, the play's important to her," Karen reminded him.

Sid shrugged. "She didn't look so interested a minute ago."

A horn beeped outside the house. Sid stiffened and automatically rose to his feet.

"There's Buzzy," Diana said. "Daddy?"

"Diana, I didn't let Eric go around the corner," he answered.

She turned to her mother. "Mom, please!"

"Sid, she'll be in a car with other kids."

"Daddy!"

Sid sighed, then nodded. "All right. You win this time, sweetheart. But come straight home afterward. No stops. *None*! If the others want to stop some place, call me and I'll pick you up."

"Thanks. I love ya, Daddy! Bye!" She breezed from the living room.

Karen walked to the window. "It's Buzzy all right, and five or six others, all jammed into his Beetle. None on motorcycles, I'll have you know."

Karen turned from the window as the Beetle puttered away with the voices of the kids drowning out the engine.

"Gary, we should be going," Val said, standing.

He got up. "You sure you don't want to go over this first?" Gary asked, brandishing the envelope. "Some of it's pretty crazy."

"Crazy sells," Sid said absently. "But that doesn't mean I'll do it. No, really. You take care of it. That's what comes from being so efficient.

More responsibility.''

"Okay," Gary said. "You know my thinking. No gimmicks, just an emphasis on Fairgate service, and the extra full-year warranty."

"Fine—that's just fine, Gary." Sid appeared to be barely listening, his forehead knit with agitation and worry.

"Congratulations again on the baby," Val said.

"Thanks." Karen ached seeing Sid's distress. "I'll just be glad when I'm sure those thugs have finally left Knots Landing. Until then I won't be able to concentrate on having a baby or anything else."

"As the lady says—tomorrow is another day," Gary offered.

"I can't wait," Sid uttered dismally.

"Oh Sid," Karen said, and punched him lightly.

As Sid opened the front door, headlights shone in his eyes and tires screeched down the cul-de-sac toward him. The horn blasted steadily.

Sid walked out onto the porch, with Karen and the Ewings standing behind him. Buzzy's Beetle sped into the circle, spun to the curb, then halted as Buzzy leapt from the car and raced up to the house toward the adults.

"Buzzy!" Karen cried out.

"What're you doing back here?" Sid asked angrily.

"Mr. Fairgate," the boy said, panting as he approached the house, "Mr. Fairgate, he took her!"

"What?" Karen demanded.

"He ran me off the road, then grabbed Diana

and took her, right outside the circle. He was waiting for us!''

''Who?'' Sid asked.

''Some guy on a motorcycle. He had a beard.''

''Oh God!'' Karen moaned.

''Where?''

''Down the boulevard. Right at the foot of the hill.'' Buzzy's words were breathy. ''They headed for the beach. We tried to stop him but couldn't.''

Sid dashed toward the car.

''I'll call the police!'' Karen called, as Gary ran after Sid.

Sid had the car backed down the driveway before Gary could reach him, and Ewing watched as Sid drove off. He turned and ran for his car next door.

''Gary!'' Val shouted.

''Call Kenny and Richard!'' he yelled back, then jumped into his car.

Val ran home.

One, two, three. Breathe slowly, Diana told herself. She shrank from contact with the smelly biker who held her imprisoned on his motorcycle. The man had pulled her from Buzzy's car before she knew what was happening, thrust her down on the bike's seat, sat behind her, pinned her to him, then took off.

''Almost there.'' The biker's breath was hot against her ear. ''You know, you're one sexy broad. I'm gonna enjoy this.''

''Let me go!'' Diana seethed.

''Nothin' doin','' he said. ''You're my revenge. And revenge is sweet!'' He smacked his lips. "You're not going anywhere." He squeezed his legs around her thighs, then firmed up his grip around her stomach.

Diana couldn't move. "No! Let me go!" She elbowed his sides and tried to wriggle free from his arm.

"No you don't," he spat, and twisted her arm behind her back while he juggled the handlebars with his other hand.

Diana winced. "You're hurting me!"

"That's nothin'," the man warned. "*Nothin'* compared to what I'll do to you if you try anything smart, girlie. Got that?" he screamed into her ear.

Diana was silent. Too scared to try to move, she sat as firmly as she could on the motorcycle, and felt sickened by the feel of the man pressing up against her.

They followed the familiar route to the beach. As they rode Diana's eyes frantically searched the roads for a patrol car, but she saw none.

The biker turned down the road into the beach parking lot, then onto the ramp that led down to the sand. Below her as they descended Diana saw flames and shadows, but nothing more.

The biker finally stopped his machine next to the flaming trash can. The other bikers stared at her as the man effortlessly lifted Diana from the seat and put her on the sand. He wrapped an arm around her slender waist. "You just stick close to me and you won't get hurt," he said. "But you try anything—" He abruptly tightened his arm.

"I won't," Diana gasped. "Believe me, I won't." She shivered as the wind whipped the flames up from the trash can in a funnel of fire.

The breeze suddenly shifted and thick smoke blew toward her. Diana coughed and hugged herself as the biker led her to a blanket nearby.

"What—what're you gonna do with me?" she stuttered.

The man leered in the pale firelight.

"No!" Diana screamed. She struggled from his hands, freed herself, then fell onto the sand.

The biker laughed maliciously.

"Hey, Alien, can't control her?" a voice called out.

"No problem."

Diana scrambled up to her feet but felt the biker's hand on her back. She wrenched from it and took another step before he pulled her back. Diana slammed against his body. He held her tightly to him, looking down at her face, then laughed.

"Come on," he said with raw menace. "I told you what would happen if you tried anything."

"What?" Her face felt frozen with terror.

"Never mind. Just sit on the blanket. Shouldn't be long now."

"What are you talking about?" Diana asked. "Why'd you take me?"

"You ask too many questions," Alien retorted.

"Are you trying to get back at my mother? Is this some kind of revenge for her throwing you in jail?"

"Yeah, that's right," Alien said. "You're a real little genius, you know that?"

"That stinks, like you," Diana exploded.

He threw her down on the blanket. "Keep your mouth shut—this'll all be over soon."

Diana stared up at him glumly. "Great. Just

what I wanted to hear.''

"Shut your mouth!" Alien bellowed.

"Oh God, I wish I'd never tried out for that dumb play," Diana muttered.

Alien slapped her face, hard enough to send her reeling backward. "I'm not kiddin'!"

"Okay, okay," Diana snapped, settling down on the blanket.

Alien stood watching her for a minute, scanned the parking lot above them, then pulled out a pack of cigarettes and squatted next to her. "Hey," he said in a strangely casual voice, offering the pack. "Want one?"

"No," Diana said. "I don't smoke."

Alien shrugged and lit up. "How old are you anyway?" he asked, exhaling a snake of smoke.

"I thought you told me not to talk," she said icily, then watched the phosphorescent waves crash and recede on the sand.

Chapter Thirteen

Rescue

Damn, Sid Fairgate thought as he blasted his car out of Seaview Circle and on toward the beach. I must have been insane to let her go. Crazy. I just let her sweet-talk me into giving her permission. But hell, how could I know that the bikers would yank her out of Buzzy's car? How could I know they'd take her?

His forehead started to sweat profusely. Sid wiped it with the back of his hand as he drove recklessly, cutting corners too sharply, his tires losing layers of rubber as he turned.

Just let me get there in time, please, let me save Diana. If they've hurt her—if they've laid a finger on my daughter, I'll beat them into the sand until they'll never hurt anybody again. No one hurts someone I love!

Sid sped along the winding road that led down to the beach. As he turned into the parking lot he saw a small point of light below—a fire of some kind on the sand. That's them, he thought. That must be them.

Please, please let me be in time!

Diana pulled her coat more tightly around her as she stood next to the flaming trashcan on the beach. She was cold, nervous, but no longer as frightened. The bikers hadn't touched her. Why not?

"My dad'll be coming here to get me any minute," she assured Alien.

"We're counting on just that, sweetheart!" Music chuckled as he walked up into the ring of firelight. "Yeah, that's why we nabbed you. Didn't you know that?"

"No, I—what are you going to do to my dad?" Diana's eyes narrowed.

"You'll find out soon enough," Music said.

A car screeched into the parking lot above them, headlights shining.

"Someone's sure in a hurry," Alien laughed.

Music whistled as he approached them. "That citizen musta broke the law to get here so fast." He slapped Alien's back. "Shocking, isn't it?"

"Yeah," the bearded biker said.

"Mary, Alison, grab her," Alien ordered.

"No!" Diana flailed her arms.

The two women locked their hands around Diana's wrists, immobilizing her.

Diana struggled to break free from them.

"Just stand there," Mary barked. "Don't try anything." She looked at Music. "What're you gonna do?"

"Shut up." He turned and crossed his arms, watching the car move in the parking lot. "Come on, guys. Let's throw up some defense here. But don't touch him—he's all mine."

The bikers straggled over to him, forming a haphazard wall between Diana and the parking lot.

Footsteps pounded down the ramp and echoed on the beach. Seconds later, Sid Fairgate ran up to the fire. He spotted Diana.

"You okay?" he asked urgently, staring at Alien and Music.

"I'm fine, Daddy," Diana said.

"Good." Sid was out of breath, but he stepped forward and pushed Music savagely backward, catching the man off guard. The biker stumbled and fell to the sand. Sid walked past him, gripped Diana's hand above Mary's fingers and jerked his daughter out of the women's grasp.

"Hey!" Mary whined. "That hurt!"

Music shook his head, still sitting on the sand.

"We're leaving." Sid walked toward the ramp, leading Diana along with him.

"No, you're not!" Music started to rise to his feet.

Sid swung Diana to his other side, turned and jumped on the downed biker. Sid locked his hands around Music's neck and applied pressure.

"Hey! Nobody beats up on my buddy!" Alien ranted, and pounced on Sid's back. He lifted him from Music. "Hear me?"

Before the big man could throw a punch Sid twisted free from his control and staggered toward Diana, who stood half-way to the parking lot. Then Music took a flying dive and grabbed Sid's ankles just before he hit the sand.

"Let me go, punk!" Sid said, savagely kicking

Music's hands away.

As Alien approached, Sid dug his shoes into Music's arms, producing a howl of pain from the man, then scrambled to his feet. Without hesitation he plowed his fist into Alien's ample stomach. The big man grunted as Sid blasted another punch into his jaw.

"Shouldn't we help out?" Ross asked. "Come on, Music—let's tear this guy up!"

"Everyone else stay back!" Music commanded, waving his hands at his fellow bikers. Blood oozed from his lip. "We can take care of this guy alone."

Alien reeled under the pain caused by Sid's fist.

"You *bastard*!" Music slowly approached Sid.

"Come on, punk. Try it." Sid wiped sweat from his brow and confidently took a fighter's stance. "I'll wipe you from the face of the earth. No one threatens my family."

"Yeah?" Music sneered and then spit. "Here it comes, man!" He threw a punch which Sid easily deflected.

Alien stood, shaking his head groggily. "Hey, man," he groaned. "Bad karma."

Sid noticed movement in the darkness behind Music.

"Two against one aren't fair odds in my book," Gary Ewing said.

Music spun around. "Who the hell are you?"

Gary bodily lifted the man from the sand and threw him. He landed five feet away with a yelp. Ewing walked to him and drove his foot into Music's side.

"Thanks, Gary!" Sid warily eyed the other

bikers, but they hung back—apparently following Music's orders. He turned and, seeing Alien lurch forward, powered his fist into the man's hairy chin.

Headlights flashed above them in the parking lot. Sid hoped it was more help. Gary, meanwhile, had dropped to his knees on Music's chest. The biker gasped as his lungs emptied under the tall man's weight.

"Get the hell offa me, man!" Music sputtered. "Come on!"

"Hey, maybe we should help them out," one of the bikers said, as he nervously watched Sid and Gary systematically tear Music and Alien apart.

"No way," Ross decided. "Man, those guys look like they feel no pain!"

Rage exploded through Sid's body as he pummelled the biker. The sea breezes, the pounding of the ocean, the firelight and the rest of the world dimmed as he poured his concentration and physical strength into hurting the man. After a few seconds he glanced up and saw Gary Ewing punching out Music. Good, he thought. Two almost down.

"Diana!" Richard Avery yelled as he ran down the ramp with Kenny Ward, who held a jack handle that shone in the firelight. "Are you hurt?"

"No," she said, and turned to see the familiar faces. Behind them she saw another moving figure.

"Diana?" a woman's thin voice cried out.

"Mom!" She ran toward the shadow.

As they saw Richard and Kenny approach, the

remaining five standing bikers—three men, two women—moved even closer together.

"Let's get them!" one of them said.

Ross looked down at Music and Alien and shrugged. "Oh hell, why not?"

"Naw, those squares aren't worth the effort," Mary said.

"Come on, man! Let's help Music and Alien out!"

As Kenny and Richard approached the group Ross tried to pull Gary from Music, who lay half-conscious on the sand, dark splotches surrounding his face. Gary turned and his fist solidly connected with Ross's chin. The man went spinning backwards.

"You okay?" Richard asked Sid, who stood over Alien.

"Fine. Get the others!"

A curly-headed biker suddenly linked Sid's arms behind his back and tried to push him onto his knees. With his elbows, Sid jabbed the biker in the ribs.

"Diana, are you all right?" Karen cried as she embraced her daughter. The wind whipped her hair and clothing as she repeatedly stroked Diana's hair.

"Yes, I'm fine, Mom," Diana said. "They didn't touch me. They just used me to get you here."

"Me?" Karen said, shaking her head.

Richard Avery's fist landed hard on Curly's back. The man moaned and rolled away in pain.

Kenny, meanwhile, moved in on another one. The biker flung his jack handle, missed his running target, and cursed. Kenny sped down the sand after him. The biker stopped short and turned, ready for a confrontation. He flicked a switchblade from his back pocket.

Kenny stood still. "Whoa!" he said.

"You fight? You die," the biker threatened, his face dark in the moonlight.

Red, blue and white lights charged the mist with color as three police cars pulled into the beach parking lot.

"Damn!" the biker stormed, and hurled the knife at Kenny, who flattened himself on the sand just as the knife pierced the ground a foot behind him.

Farther up on the beach Gary Ewing pushed himself backwards onto his feet and stared down at Sid. "That's enough," he said.

Sid looked up from where he'd resumed beating Alien. "What?"

"That's enough. He's not going anywhere."

Sid nodded grudgingly and stumbled away from Alien. The man lay barely conscious, his face bleeding in several places, the fingers of one hand jerking.

"Anybody else?" Sid asked, as he surveyed the scene.

The two girls were gone. Alien and Music lay on the ground, motionless. The curly-topped biker sat on the sand, obviously incapable of further violence. Ross had apparently slipped away as well. A few yards away, Sid's wife and daughter were holding each other tightly. Richard Avery stood, hands on his hips, next to the fire. Kenny was nowhere in sight.

"Sid!" Karen called. "Are you okay?"

"I'm fine," he said. A scarlet line trickled

down from a cut near his chin.

As six policemen hurried down the ramp toward the melee, Karen and Diana ran over to Sid and they all hugged.

Back in the surf Kenny grabbed a clump of slick, wet seaweed and hurled it at the rapidly departing biker. The long strands wrapped around the man's head.

"Damn you!" the biker yelled. "I can't see!"

Kenny worked the man over and then dragged him, his head still encased in seaweed, toward the fire and the growing crowd that gathered there.

Sid turned back to stare at the spot where Music and Alien lay on the sand. Reluctantly releasing him, Karen held onto her daughter as she watched Sid approach the two prone men.

Gary Ewing kicked Alien over to lie next to Music.

Sid stared down at them. "If either of you," he said, gasping for breath, "ever lays a hand on anybody I love again . . ." He rapidly inhaled and wiped his face. His hand reddened.

Sergeant Willis ran up and shook his head at the scene. "I take it these are the ones who've been bothering you?" he asked, indicating the downed bikers.

Sid nodded. "Some of them."

Kenny walked up with the biker he had captured and threw him down on the ground on top of Music and Alien, who groaned when he landed.

"Some of them got away," Kenny informed the group.

"We know," Sid sighed and wiped the blood

from his face with the back of his fist.

"We'll take these boys in now," Willis said. "You can wait till morning to file your charges if you want. I'd certainly understand."

Richard brushed sand from his coat. "I can start right now," he said. "Kidnapping. Assault. Intent to do bodily harm." Richard turned to Diana. "Anything else I should mention?"

She looked at him blank-faced, then her eyes widened. Diana shook her head.

"Did they try?" he asked.

"They hinted. That's all."

"Conspiracy!" Richard's eyes gleamed in the dwindling fire. "I should be able to think up ten or twelve more by morning. We tried to give them a break, but some people have to learn the hard way."

"I'd say they're off to a good start," Willis said wryly. "Get them out of here, men."

His officers bustled around with riot cuffs.

"Did they hurt you, Daddy?" Diana asked as her family headed up the ramp.

"No, baby, I'm fine. Really."

Karen turned back toward the shore. "How about everybody else? Everyone okay?"

"Okay?" Richard grinned. "I feel *great*. Can you believe that? Great!"

Kenny and Gary joined him and they walked with the Fairgates back to the parking lot.

"What a fight!" Richard seemed to savor his words.

Sid smiled with satisfaction. "We showed those punks."

"I'm just glad it's over." Karen shivered beside her husband.

"I'll bet Alien's glad it's over, too," Diana said happily. As they reached the top of the ramp Diana looked down at the beach. The fire had nearly died, the flames dipping low and then momentarily flaring. In the silvery starlight the police hustled the bikers across the sand to the ramp.

She turned toward the car and hurried to catch up with her parents.

"What a night!" she cried, and hugged them tightly.

Chapter Fourteen
The Cradle Will Fall

"What's he look like?" the fourteen-year-old girl asked as she and Ginger drove home from the movies.

"Well, Jill, he's almost fifteen, kinda tall, hair down to his eyes and—you know. Cute."

"Yeah. But just because I'm visiting, you don't have to introduce me to boys." Jill was blonde, slim, with an attractive, intelligent face.

"I know, Sis. I just thought you might like to get to know him better."

"Why?"

"Well, for starters—he plays basketball."

Jill glanced at Ginger. "He plays basketball?"

"Uh-huh." Ginger turned onto the street that led to Seaview Circle. "I've watched him practice for hours in his driveway, alone or sometimes with friends."

"Is he any good?" Jill's voice was clipped, cool.

"I'm no expert, but I'd say yeah, he's good."

Jill thought for a moment, then shrugged. "Okay, Ginger. Just don't tell Mom you set me up with some wild boy the day I got here."

Ginger laughed. "Hey, there he is." She pointed down the road ahead.

"Where?"

"See? On that bike. He's turning down Seaview Circle."

"Oh, yeah." Jill arched her eyebrows. "Oh, wow!"

"Jill! If Dad could hear you say things like that!"

"He can't," she said quickly, studying Eric.

"Hey, Eric!" Ginger called out as they drove up beside the bicycling boy.

"Hi, Mrs. Ward!" Eric waved.

"Meet you there, okay?" Ginger pointed to her driveway.

Eric nodded and rode to it.

When he was gone, Ginger turned to Jill. "What do you think, little sister?"

"Not bad," she considered. "Better than I'd hope for one of your neighborhood's boys."

Ginger smiled. "I thought so. She pulled up onto her driveway, three houses down the circle from Sid and Karen's home, and turned off the engine.

Eric lowered his bike to the curb and walked up, hands in his pockets, His eyes widened as Jill stepped from Ginger's car

"Eric, this is my sister, Jill."

"Hi," the girl said.

"Hi." Eric's voice was breathy. He looked warily at Jill, taken aback but obviously pleased with what he saw.

"I've told you about each other." Ginger's manner was nonchalant. "Jill's staying the weekend with Kenny and me."

"Oh . . . good," Eric murmured. He pulled his hands from his pockets and held them awkwardly at his sides. The boy avoided both pairs of eyes, except for momentary glances to ensure that they were still looking at him.

Ginger's mouth turned up in a faint smile.

"So, maybe you two can do something together. Spend some time having fun while she's here this weekend. Get to know each other."

"If you're not already busy this weekend," Jill added quickly. "I'll understand if—"

"No, ah, I'm not busy." Eric peered out from behind the dark hair that obscured one eye and half the other. "Not at all. Nothing I can't get out of, I mean." He pushed his hair back and looked openmouthed at Jill for a moment, then grinned sheepishly and crossed his arms.

"Good. I hoped you two could be friends." Ginger's eyes twinkled. "Just don't disappear without telling me. Our parents would kill me if I let anything happen to you out here," Ginger said to Jill.

"It won't," the girl replied coolly.

Ginger glanced at Eric. "Bye!" She went to her front door and fumbled for her keys.

Eric looked at Jill for a long moment, silent, then looked down at his bike. "You wanna go somewhere?"

"Sure," she said. "How?"

"You could borrow my sister's bike," Eric suggested.

"Thanks. Where do you want to go?" Jill asked brightly.

"I don't know. I can't think of anywhere to go." Eric squinted and bit his lip slightly.

Jill half-smiled and perused the cul-de-sac. "Nice neighborhood."

"Thanks. I like it." Eric thrust out his chest, imitating a home owner's pride.

She laughed. "Which house is yours?"

"That one," Eric pointed to the largest house—a two-story massive structure at the end of Seaview Circle.

Jill looked very pleased. "Good. I was hoping that you'd say that."

"Why?" He eyed her uncertainly.

"Because of that basket hoop over the garage door." She turned back to him. "Do you play?"

"Basketball?"

"Yes."

Eric shrugged. "Sure. You like basketball?" he asked, with an expression of amazement.

"I love it. In fact, I can't think of a better way to spend a Saturday afternoon. Can you?"

Eric shook his head, dazed.

"Want to play a little one-on-one?" Jill dramatically straightened her posture to emphasize the challenge.

"You and me?" Eric was still disbelieving.

"Sure. Why not?"

"Well, because—" Eric didn't know what else to say.

"Because why? Afraid I'll beat you?" Jill teased lightly.

"No . . ."

"Then do you want to play or not, Eric?" She

stood before him, smiling, waiting for him to make a decision.

Now Eric straightened up too. "Sure."

"Great!" Jill looked down at her blouse and shorts. "I guess I don't need to change before we play."

"I'll get my ball." Eric walked quickly to his bike, rode to his house, and disappeared inside.

While he was gone Jill sauntered over to the Fairgate home and waited for him.

Eric soon reappeared, slightly out of breath, and rushed up to her.

"What took you so long?" Jill stood, arms crossed, leaning against the Fairgate's mailbox.

"I—" he began, then smiled.

"Let's play."

"Okay," Eric said. "Only—"

"No only's. Just play." She ran to the driveway and stood defensively beneath the net, bent low, feet wide apart on the concrete. "Just try it, Eric Fairgate!" Jill said with mock savagery. "Just try to dunk that ball through the hoop!"

Eric laughed and ran toward her.

"How about going out to dinner tonight, honey?" Sid asked as he touched his wife's arm. They sat in the kitchen drinking coffee in the early afternoon.

She looked up from her cup and smiled. "Sure. I'd love it. We really do need a celebration, now that those people are finally gone."

"I agree," Sid said gently, and bent to kiss her. As his lips touched hers a metallic clanging radiated from the garage.

"Eric," he concluded. "I'll go tell him to lay off practice for a while. That kid's driving me nuts!"

"No, let him," Karen said. She rose from the table and walked to the living room window. "He's not playing alone," she added cryptically.

"One of the neighborhood boys?" Sid asked, uninterested.

"No. It's a girl."

Sid chuckled. "Really?"

"Yes. And she's not bad."

More thuds and crashes from the driveway.

"You sure that noise isn't too much for you this afternoon?"Sid sounded concerned.

"Yes. Just because I'm pregnant doesn't mean I can't listen to my son practicing basketball with an attractive girl." She continued to look out the window. "I wonder who she is."

"Does she look like Ginger?" Sid got up from the table and walked to the window.

"Ginger? There may be a resemblance."

Sid peered out the window. "Definitely. That's Jill, Ginger's sister. She's visiting this weekend. Don't you remember she told us?"

Karen smiled. "That's right. I'd forgotten. They seem to be hitting it off."

"They're hitting something," Sid said, amused, as the house reverberated again.

"She's awfully pretty."

"Sure," Sid agreed. "But Eric's not really playing. He's letting her walk all over him. Let me go talk to that boy—"

"No, Sid. Let him do it. He's nearly grown up." Karen's eyes flooded momentarily as she turned from the window and walked back to her coffee.

Jill shot behind Eric, dribbling the basketball. Before Eric could block her, she drove up for the basket and slammed the ball against the backboard. She frowned as the ball slipped down through the net.

Eric stared at the ball, then at Jill, his face incredulous. "Hey, you're good!" he allowed.

She darted past him and bounced the ball up into her hands. "Eric, I thought you said you wanted to play basketball."

"I do."

"But you're just standing around. You're not guarding me or anything. This isn't any fun at all."

Eric looked at the ground and shrugged. "I don't know . . . I mean, you're a girl and everything."

"A girl and everything?" Jill repeated. "So what? You afraid of hurting me?"

Eric nodded, then shook his head. "Not exactly."

"You haven't come within a foot of me. There's no way you could hurt me."

"Look, Jill—"

"No, Eric. This'll be boring unless we get one thing straight right from the start."

"What's that?"

"Forget I'm a girl. Okay? If we're going to play, let's *play*!"

Eric looked at her with awe. "Okay."

Jill dribbled to the back of the driveway, then moved inbounds, directly toward a guarding Eric. The young man darted to block her access to the basket.

"Hah!" Jill said.

Eric swatted at the ball, moving with the girl, playing as he would against any boy.

"That's more like it, Eric!" Jill encouraged him, and dribbled up for yet another shot at the basket.

Karen ran the brush through her hair as she sat before the mirror, luxuriating in the moment of peace. The bikers were in jail or long gone. She was happily, joyfully pregnant and couldn't wait to see her baby. She had no more problems or decisions to make in the immediate future.

She stopped brushing and stared into her reflected eyes. Had she changed since her pregnancy? Karen studied herself, then patted herself on the cheek and smiled. No. Not as far as she could tell.

As she rose from the chair Karen doubled over and sat down hard again. Electric pains spiraled inside her abdomen. She gasped, the pain momentarily shocking her respiratory system into nonaction.

Karen put a hand to her mouth and breathed deeply as she waited for the pain to vanish. A moment later it dimmed and then faded into a barely perceptible throb. Seconds later she felt fine again.

Karen puffed and looked in the mirror again. What was that? What could have caused so much pain? She pressed her lips together. Probably just the tension of the last few days. She might have pulled a muscle or something in all the excitement.

Karen checked her appearance one last time, then rose and left the bedroom.

"Honey, about ready?" Sid called from downstairs.

"Just about," she called back. Karen slipped on a sleek black satin coat and walked down.

Sid whistled as she made her entrance.

"Whew!" He reeled. "Look at that!"

"Wow!" Michael was impressed too.

"How often do we celebrate a new baby and the end of a motorcycle gang?" Karen giggled.

Sid kissed her cheek. "Are we ready?" He surveyed Eric, Michael and Diana. The boys wore suits, and Diana an expensive, elegant blue silk dress. All were waiting impatiently.

"Yes!" Diana said emphatically.

"Let's go. I'm starved," Karen agreed.

A half-hour later the stiff-lipped waiter served the Fairgates their meal. Diana looked at Michael as he surveyed his chicken.

"You know which fork to use, right?"

Michael looked down at his place setting. Before him lay three forks, and an assortment of other cutlery. "A fork's a fork," he said uncertainly.

"Honestly, Michael," Diana muttered, exasperated. "You're going to embarrass me in front of all these people."

"Michael, Diana, that's enough," Sid scolded gently.

Karen speared a piece of steamed broccoli with her fork and lifted it to her mouth. She chewed the vegetable slowly and swallowed it.

"This is delicious, isn't it, honey?" Sid asked.

"Yes." She smiled back at him.

"Michael!" Diana said.

The boy sat digging into his chicken breast with

two forks, pulling the tender flesh from the bones with one while holding the bird still with the other.

"A knife and a fork, not a fork and a fork!" Diana was mortified.

"That's great, Michael!" Eric cheered him on.

"This is working fine, Mom." Michael looked up at Karen.

She stared at him, then shrugged to Sid. "Maybe he's got a point."

Sid frowned. "Are you feeling okay, honey? You seem a bit tense."

"I'm fine," she replied warmly. "Just all the excitement, I guess." She picked at the broccoli on her plate, then set her fork down and sat very still. Karen lifted her wine glass and held it. She couldn't eat another bite.

Sid leaned across the table and clinked his glass with hers. "To you, darling," he said.

Karen smiled almost shyly and lifted her glass to his. "To us."

They drank, while Sid studied Karen's eyes. He broke their contact by looking at the kids. Sid raised his glass to them. "Here's mud in your eye."

The kids laughed and drank their soda.

Karen felt the searing pain begin again and gain momentum. With a herculean effort she rose suddenly from the table. "Excuse me," she said, and turned and left.

She went to the ladies' lounge and collapsed on the crushed yellow velvet couch.

Sid stared after Karen as she left, but he tried not to worry. Pregnancies have strange side effects, remembered Karen's earlier years.

"How was Buzzy yesterday?" Michael asked Diana.

"You shut up!" she warned.

"You love him!" Michael stuck his tongue out at her.

"That's none of your business, Michael!" she snapped, her face red. Diana shifted her attention toward Eric, who sat quietly eating. "And I suppose *you* think we're getting married."

He looked up at her quickly. "No—ah, I wasn't listening. What did you say?"

Michael sneered. "Eric's in love with Jill. He played basketball with her all afternoon."

"Kids," Sid began to referee.

"Mr. Fairgate, excuse me, but it's your wife—" a waitress said in a low voice as she bent near the table. "She needs you."

Sid pushed back his chair and followed her through the maze of tables to the reception desk. He felt his balance shift slightly, and knew it wasn't the wine. Something was very wrong—Karen was in trouble.

Karen stood leaning against the reception desk, her face pallid and drawn, her skin moist with perspiration.

"Honey, what is it? What can I do?" Sid cringed at his wife's obvious anguish.

"I just phoned Dr. Bender." Karen's voice was wan. "We've got to get to the hospital, Sid. We've got to!"

Sid stared at her for a split second, then fished for his car keys as the kids came up to them.

The trip was short but hectic. Karen sat stiffly

upright on the seat, but Sid observed waves of pain pass over her face. She used all of her will power in trying to mask the sensations, but she could not succeed.

The kids were strangely quiet on the trip. Twice Sid glanced in the rear view mirror to ensure that he hadn't forgotten them in his haste. Their bodies were rigid, their faces ghostlike in the dim light.

"Hello, Mrs. Fairgate," Dr. Bender greeted her as they met in the emergency room entrance. "This way."

She wheeled Karen down a corridor and waved to Sid to tell him not to follow.

Frustrated, he turned back to where the kids stood beside a rack of booklets filled with medical information and advertisements from pharmaceutical companies.

"We have a while to wait, I'd say," Sid said.

"Of course." Diana seemed far older than her sixteen years.

Michael and Eric stood motionless, hands stuffed into their pockets, eyes downward.

Fifteen minutes later Val and Gary Ewing joined Sid and the children in the waiting room.

"Thanks for coming." Sid already had the appearance of a man who had not slept for days, his eyes circled with gray shadows.

"I'm glad you called. I'm sorry about—" Val began.

"Thanks," Sid covered her words quickly.

"How are the kids taking it?" Gary asked.

"As well as can be expected." They moved farther down the corridor.

"I'm not worried about them," Gary said.

"I'm worried about you. You look terrible, Sid—just awful."

"Thanks." Sid tried to manage a weak smile. "I thought the kids ought to get some sleep. Just because I won't doesn't mean the rest of the family shouldn't."

"We'll drive them home," Val offered.

"Thanks." He pressed his forehead with his fingertips. "I don't know. Dr. Bender's been in there with Karen for quite a while. We should have heard something by now." His hand moved through his hair.

"I'm sure everything will be fine," Val assured him. "Don't you worry."

"I appreciate your help."

"It's the least we can do, Sid," Gary said soothingly, and put an arm around his shoulder.

Diana rose from the plastic couch and approached her father. "I don't want to leave, Daddy," she pleaded. "I can't. I want to know what's happening."

Sid hugged her to him. "Honey, there's nothing you can do, and they're not telling me anything."

"I want to wait here with you. Please, Dad."

"I'm sorry. Go on home and get some sleep. You've got to look after your brothers too. Okay?"

She sighed. "All right . . ." Diana reluctantly turned back to where Michael was resting on the couch. She gently roused him.

"Sid, I—" Val touched Sid's hand.

"I know. You don't have to say it. Thanks for your help."

Sid briefly embraced both boys and sent them

off with Gary and Val. He waved and tried to smile hopefully as Diana looked back at him. Once they were gone Sid collapsed onto a chair. His face twisted with sorrow and he blinked repeatedly, fighting back unfamiliar, stinging tears.

He sat for a half hour, finally letting his head drop back to lean against the hospital wall.

"Mr. Fairgate?"

Sid opened his eyes and looked up. "Dr. Bender. Did she lose—" he said anxiously, rising.

The doctor nodded. "She's fine now. I gave her a sedative and she's sleeping comfortably."

"Thank God she's all right," he sighed. "When can she go home?" Sid's body was limp with relief and sadness.

"First thing in the morning," Dr. Bender promised. "She'll be just fine by then."

Sid nodded numbly and automatically started to sit down again. Halfway through his motion he changed his mind and looked at the doctor.

"Can I see her?"

The doctor pointed down the corridor. "Room two-thirteen," she said.

"Thanks, Dr. Bender."

She nodded and walked away, her sensible shoes creaking softly on the linoleum.

Sid turned toward room two-thirteen. Just five rooms to the left—Karen was there. He slowed his pace, realizing he was nearly running. Upon reaching the door Sid stopped and took a deep breath, expelling the air with a faint whistle. He then walked inside.

Karen lay on her back, wrapped in a white

hospital gown, blue blankets up around her chin. Her hair spread out around her head like a silky nimbus on the starched pillow. She looked ashen but her face was calm.

Sid settled into the chair beside the bed and watched his wife sleep away her pain. After a moment his own head nodded.

Sid straightened his spine. Have to keep awake, he told himself. Have to stay awake. Too much to think about!

So our plans didn't work out this time, Sid thought. That's okay. We'll just have to make some new ones. I won't really miss this chance— or will I?

Sid Fairgate gazed at his wife. You're some kind of remarkable woman, you know that, Karen Fairgate? You fight off a gang of motorcycle thugs and lose a baby all within the same week, and yet you still look peaceful, beautiful, and wonderfully alive.

His eyelids seemed to lower of their own accord as he considered the future. The images that entered his mind seemed to drug him, and Sid fell into a deep, dreamless sleep.

He awoke with a start five minutes later. Glancing at his watch and peeking at Karen, he tiptoed from her room and walked down the hall until he found a telephone. He quickly dialed home.

"Diana? It's your dad," he said.

"Hi, Daddy!" Diana seemed fully awake. "How is Mom? I was worried about her."

"Dr. Bender said she's fine."

"Really?" Diana asked. "She looked awfully sick by the time we got to the hospital."

"She's fine."

"Super! When is she coming home?"

"I'm bringing her home in the morning."

"Great! Daddy," Diana said.

"Yes?"

"Did she—well, did she—lose the baby?"

Sid was silent for a moment.

"Did she?"

"Yes," he said softly.

"Oh, I'm—I'm sorry! I'm so sorry!" Diana cried. "I really am. I didn't mean all those things I said!"

"I know, honey—we know that," Sid said. "Don't worry about it. She's fine now, and I'll see you in the morning. Okay?"

"Okay, Daddy. And thanks for calling. I hoped you wouldn't forget."

"Not a chance, sweetheart. Good night."

He set down the receiver and walked back to room two-thirteen, half hoping to find Karen awake. When he found her slumbering Sid yawned and moved his chair flush against the bed. Flowers, he thought dimly as he began to doze. There should be flowers in the room.

He realized that by the time he could buy her flowers she'd be home. Anyway, flowers were only a symbol of his love for her. He could show her that love the minute she awoke. As long as the hospital allowed him to stay he intended to be at Karen's side.

The flowers could wait, he figured, as long as *he* was there.

Chapter Fifteen
Homecoming

Karen opened her eyes dreamily and stirred in her bed. A dull ache reminded her why she wasn't at home in her own bedroom with Sid. But I feel okay, she thought. Not great, but okay.

She noticed Sid asleep in the chair beside her and smiled at him. Poor Sid—I've really put you through the wringer, haven't I? First I make a gang mad at the whole neighborhood, then they kidnap our daughter and now I lose our baby.

The thoughts rushed by. Karen closed her eyes, trying to shut them out, but repeated images of cradles and babies invaded her mind. She tried to return to sleep.

After a few moments Karen sighed and examined the room again. She'd slept long enough, she decided, then yawned, feeling the effects of the sedative she didn't remember receiving.

She knew what Sid would ask when he woke up. "How do you feel?" he'd ask, and scrutinize her face for clues.

How *do* I feel? *What* do I feel? She had never imagined that she might lose the baby. That had never seemed a possibility to her. Conflicting emotions engulfed her.

"Honey?" Sid murmured, lifting his head from its groggy slump.

"Hello, sweetheart." Karen smiled at her husband.

He stretched his shoulders and yawned. "How are you feeling?" He studied her as she lay there.

Karen shrugged. "That's just what I was trying to figure out. I don't know. Physically, I feel fine. But otherwise—" She bit her lower lip. "I don't know."

"Are you in pain?" Sid asked tenderly.

"No. Just an ache, that's all. I can ignore it." She yawned. "What time is it? Was I asleep long?"

"It's a little after seven," Sid answered after checking his watch. "You slept about ten hours. Dr. Bender said that was the best thing you could do, so I didn't try to wake you. Even though I wanted to tell you—" Sid broke off the sentence.

She took his hand. "Sid, I had such a crazy dream. I was in this huge room." Karen closed her eyes for improved recall. "It was completely dark except for one shining candle. I kept running around the room, trying to light all the other candles that were there. But every time I'd light one, two or three others would blow out. The faster I moved, the darker the room got."

Sid placed a finger against her lips. "I'm so sorry we lost the baby, honey," he said, then kissed her head and drew back. "But we've still got so much."

Karen looked up at her husband and warmth flushed through her body—not a dangerous fever, but a primitive emotional reaction to his frankness. I've never loved him more than I do at this moment, Karen thought.

"You understand?"

"Yes, I do." Karen paused and collected her thoughts. "Sid, I'll admit it would have been fun, terrific, to have a baby. I was actually missing the diapers and the three A.M. feedings and all that."

"Yeah," Sid laughed softly. "I know. I was thinking of that a lot too."

"But it's okay that that won't be happening now, isn't it, Sid? It's not as if I don't have anything else to do."

"No question about that."

"Now I have more time to spend with the family I have. And I can keep on working to improve this world in the ways I know how."

"That's right," Sid supported her. "You've got your career." His voice was admiring, serious.

Karen smiled at him. "Thanks, Sid." She reached out for him then, lifting up slightly off her pillow.

Sid carefully wrapped her in his arms as Karen buried her face against his neck, sniffling. "Oh, Sid, you know as well as I do, I'm too old to have a baby anyway."

They kissed briefly.

"Want to go home?" Sid asked.

She brightened. "When?"

"Dr. Bender said you could leave in the morning, and it's morning."

Karen beamed. "Great! Let me get ready."

"Okay." Sid stood beside the bed. "Need any help?"

Karen's gaze was like a caress. "I have you here . . . that's all I need."

"I can't believe it!" Laura said as she sat by her bed, phone in hand. "Last night?"

"That's right," Val said at the other end. "It was all so fast—nobody seemed to know what was going on."

"Oh, poor Karen!" Laura's voice cracked. "When will she be home?"

"Today, tomorrow—I'm not really sure. I called the hospital but Karen wasn't in her room."

"Poor Karen and Sid," Laura repeated.

"After all that—" Val stopped. "'No mother should have her babies taken away from her like that."

Laura sighed. "Thanks for calling, Val. We'll have to do something special for Sid and Karen."

"Okay. You think of something, y'hear?"

"Fine. Bye."

Karen Fairgate sat uncomfortably in the wheelchair, fully dressed, as Sid pushed her down the hospital corridor toward the elevators.

"This is ridiculous, Sid," she complained. "Let me out of this chair. I feel perfectly fine."

"Hospital policy," Sid reminded her. "Enjoy it while you can. The chair stays here."

"Oh, okay." Karen tried to relax.

Sid brought the chair to a smooth halt before the elevators. He pushed the button and looked at Karen, his love for her clearly visible.

"I'm going to be glad to be home, " Karen said.

"Me too."

"It might be strange at first—my whole future's changed again overnight. But there'll be lots to do around the house. The kids always take up loads of time, and I'll bet the house is a wreck."

Sid chortled. "You've only been gone half a day, honey," he teased her.

"I know. But I also know those kids!"

The elevator doors opened. Sid and Karen stopped talking and turned to enter it. Karen's face fell as she saw the elevator's occupants.

A young couple, obviously on their way down from the maternity floor, smiled radiantly at them. The mother sat in a wheelchair, cradling her newborn, while the father stood proudly beside her.

Karen felt a surge of raw emotion shoot through her. The increasing weight of grief she'd been storing up threatened to crush her.

For a moment the two couples stared at each other, then the elevator doors shut. Sid took Karen's hand—his grip was firm, warm, strengthening.

As they drove into Seaview Circle most of its residents seemed to be outside. Richard and Laura Avery were busily washing their cars on the driveway. As Richard waved to the Fairgates the hose went wild, splashing Laura's face. She yelled, grabbed it and ran to turn off the water.

Gary and Val Ewing sat on the curb talking to each other, while Kenny and Ginger Ward

walked out from their house toward the couple.
All four waved to Karen and Sid as they passed.

As they approached their house Karen saw Eric
playing one-on-one with Jill in the Fairgate
driveway.

"Kids," Sid said with affection.

"Yes. Aren't they wonderful?" Karen
snuggled beside him. "I appreciate them even
more now."

"Looks like Eric and Jill are quite a number,"
he observed, parking along the curving curb to
allow his son's game to proceed unimpeded.

"Maybe," she said. "But she'll only be here
until tonight."

"I know." Sid watched his son dash across the
driveway. "Eric's growing up."

"They all are. Especially Diana—she's
changing faster than I can keep track of."

Sid sighed. "Maybe our lives can get back to
normal, now that the gang's locked up. It's been
rougher on you than anyone else, hasn't it?"

"I don't know," she pondered. "You've been
pretty upset lately too."

Sid turned off the engine and opened his door,
then raced around the car and opened Karen's
door. "Service with a smile." He bowed like a
chauffeur.

"Oh, Sid." Karen giggled.

He helped her rise from the seat. They walked
slowly, arm-in-arm, up to the front door.

"Hi, Mom!" Eric called as he halted his
dribbling. "This is Jill."

"Hi, Jill."

"Here." Eric handed Jill the ball and ran up to
his mother. "How are you feeling?"

"I'm fine, Eric. Really." She kissed his forehead.

He hugged her. "Good. I'm glad you're back home," he said, shyly.

"It's good to be back." She looked over at Jill.

"I hope you're feeling better, Mrs. Fairgate," the girl said.

"I feel wonderful!" Karen motioned toward the hoop. "So don't let me interrupt your game. You and Eric go ahead and play."

"Eric!" Michael came running out of the house. "You *never* let me play since you met Jill—"

"Michael, my little angel," Karen said gently.

"Mom!" He rushed to her and wrapped his arms around her, then stepped back.

"You were saying to Eric?" Karen prodded.

"Nothing. It doesn't matter." Michael looked over to the driveway. "Hi, Jill."

"Hello, Michael. If you get Diana to play we can go two-on-two," Jill offered.

Michael threw his hands up in the air. "It would be a miracle if she did *anything* I wanted her to do."

Karen and Sid laughed and continued on into the house. Once inside Karen turned to her husband.

"Sid, do the kids know?"

"Yes," he said. "I told Diana when she asked me last night on the phone. Dr. Bender didn't go into details, but she told me all I needed to know . . ."

Karen understood. "She's a great doctor. She took real good care of me."

"And now I'll take over." Sid caressed her

cheek and moved out of her way. "Want to sit down?"

"Maybe for a minute," Karen said.

"Can I get you anything, honey?"

"A glass of water?"

"Be right back."

When Sid had gone Karen leaned back into the chair and took a deep breath. I'll pull through with my family and friends, Karen decided. I *will*. I'm strong enough to handle something like this.

Obviously, it just wasn't meant to be. This time. That doesn't mean sometime in the future—well, things might be different.

She'd have to ask Dr. Bender to check her out again to make sure she was capable of having another baby. Karen reached for the phone and then laughed. It was only eight in the morning. She could wait until afternoon at least.

Sid returned with a glass of water. He handed it to her and sat down beside her, then touched her shoulders tenderly.

"Welcome home," he whispered.

"Mother! I didn't hear you come home!" Diana exclaimed as she race down the stairs.

Karen gazed at her daughter after they'd broken their embrace. "How were the boys?"

"A pain as usual," Diana sniffed, then smiled. "But *no more* than usual. You look wonderful."

"Thanks. I feel like a wreck."

"Mom, I'm—"

"Don't say it," Karen interrupted. "I'm fine now—really—and life will go on as usual."

"I know, but all those awful things I said—"

Karen hugged her daughter again. "It doesn't

matter. We all went a little crazy there for a while. You weren't any worse than the rest of us. You don't have to apologize, okay, cookie?''

Diana nodded. ''Okay.'' She kissed Karen's cheek. ''Welcome home, Mom.''

Karen took her daughter's hand in hers, then grasped Sid's with her other. As they stood before her, she felt herself begin to tremble with emotion.

''I can make it. With you guys, I know I will.'' As Karen's gaze locked on Sid, his adoring face shimmered and dissolved into a lovely watercolor dream before her tear-splashed eyes.

You can now order previous titles of *Soaps & Serials*™ Books by mail!

Just complete the order form, detach, and send together with your check or money order payable to:

Soaps & Serials™
120 Brighton Road, Box 5201
Clifton, NJ 07015-5201

- -

Please <u>circle</u> the book #'s you wish to order:

The Young and The Restless	1	2	3	4
Days of Our Lives	1	2	3	4
Guiding Light	1	2	3	4
Another World	1	2	3	4
As The World Turns	1	2	3	4
Capitol™	1	2	3	4
Dallas™	1	2	3	4
Knots Landing™	1	2	3	4

Each book is $2.50 ($3.25 in Canada).

Total number of books
circled _____ × price above = $ _____ .

Sales tax (CT residents only) $ _____ .

Shipping and Handling $ _____ .95

Total payment enclosed $ _____ .
(check or money orders only)

Name _____

Address _____ Apt# _____

City _____

State _____ Zip _____

Telephone (_____) _____
        Area code   KL4

Soaps & Serials™ Fans!

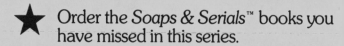

★ Order the *Soaps & Serials*™ books you have missed in this series.

★ Collect other *Soaps & Serials*™ series from their very beginnings.

★ Give *Soaps & Serials*™ series as gifts to other fans.

...see other side for ordering information

Soaps & Serials
From Pioneer Communications Network, Inc.